How the Earth Began

Scientists have studied the Sun, the stars and the rocks of the Earth to find out how the Earth formed. They think that about 4,700 million years ago the Earth did not exist. There was only an enormous cloud of dust and gases swirling round the Sun. Then the cloud split up to form several small clouds. Each of these probably became one of the planets which now go round the Sun.

1 | 4,600 MILLION YEARS AGO

The cloud which made the planet Earth began to shrink and became very hot. As it heated up it changed into a ball of liquid rock spinning in space.

2 | 4,000 MILLION YEARS AGO

Slowly, over millions of years, the ball of rock cooled down. A crust of solid rock hardened on the outside, but underneath the rock was still hot and liquid.

3 | 3,500 MILLION YEARS AGO

Thick clouds surrounded the Earth. When these cooled rain began to fall. It rained for thousands of years and the rain-water made rivers and oceans.

How life began
3,000 MILLION YEARS AGO

2,000 MILLION YEARS AGO

600 MILLION YEARS AGO

The first living things grew in the sea. They were neither animals nor plants. Scientists know very little about them because they were so tiny.

Very slowly, these tiny living things changed and became plants growing in the sea. There were no animals yet because there was no oxygen for them to breathe.

Plants make oxygen as they grow. Eventually there was enough oxygen for animals to grow in the sea. Some of the first animals were jellyfish and sponges like these.

The Fossil Clues

People who study the plants and animals which lived millions of years ago are called palaeontologists. They study fossils, which are all that remain of prehistoric life. A fossil is made when the remains of animals or plants slowly change to stone.

When scientists discover a plant or animal, they give it a Latin or Greek name so that people who speak different languages can use the same names. There is a list of what the names mean in English on the last page of this book.

Palaeontologists travel all over the world looking for fossils. When they find them they dig them out of the rock and take them back to the laboratory.

Then they study the fossil to find out what sort of plant or animal it was. Here they are measuring a giant ammonite which lived in the sea 150 million years ago.

How fossils are made

Fossils are made at the same time as the rock they are found in. Here is how it happens.

Rain and rivers wear away rocks and wash sand and mud into the sea. The sand and mud is called sediment. It slowly builds up to form thick layers on the sea floor.

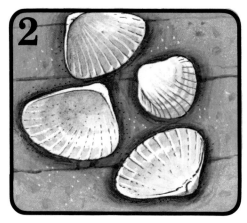

When sea creatures die their soft bodies rot away and their shells are buried in the sediment. After millions of years the layers of sediment are very deep and heavy.

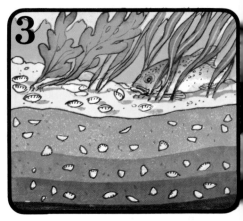

The sediment at the bottom is pressed down so hard that it becomes rock called sedimentary rock. The shells leave a print of their shape in the rock.

These prints made by shells are called fossils. Fossil prints of leaves and footprints are made like this too. Fossils of bones are made in a different way.

Bones buried in the sand are slowly dissolved away. The space left is filled by tiny grains of sand which harden into a fossil shaped like the animal's bones.

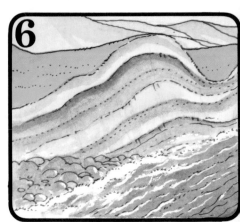

Movements in the Earth's crust lift the rocks above the sea. As the rocks wear away the fossils of plants and animals which lived long ago, appear on the surface.

Plants and animals in the rock

Here are the fossil remains of some plants and animals. They have not been drawn to scale. In this book the names of individual plants or animals are printed in *italics* and the names of groups of plants or animals are in ordinary type.

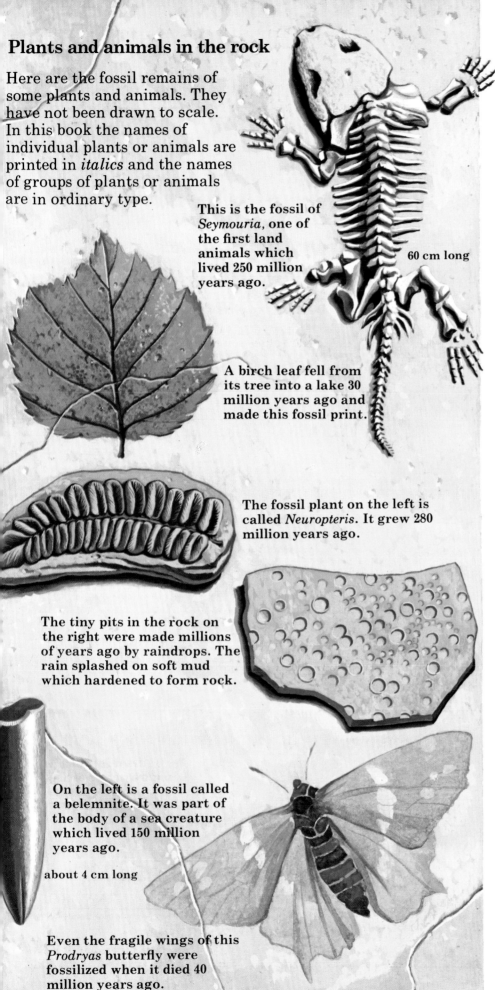

This is the fossil of *Seymouria*, one of the first land animals which lived 250 million years ago.

60 cm long

A birch leaf fell from its tree into a lake 30 million years ago and made this fossil print.

The fossil plant on the left is called *Neuropteris*. It grew 280 million years ago.

The tiny pits in the rock on the right were made millions of years ago by raindrops. The rain splashed on soft mud which hardened to form rock.

On the left is a fossil called a belemnite. It was part of the body of a sea creature which lived 150 million years ago.

about 4 cm long

Even the fragile wings of this *Prodryas* butterfly were fossilized when it died 40 million years ago.

Model fossils

You will need plaster of Paris, plasticine, thin card and some leaves.

Make a flat piece of plasticine, large enough to put the leaf on. Then make a ring of card to fit round the leaf.

Press the edge of the ring into the plasticine and put the leaf inside the ring. Press the leaf gently to make it lie flat.

Mix a thin paste of plaster of Paris and pour it over the leaf. Then leave it to set.

When the plaster is hard, take off the ring and peel away the plasticine. Gently pull the leaf off the plaster. Try making model fossils of sea-shells too.

The First Life

The land was dry and lifeless 550 million years ago. But the seas and lakes were full of plants and animals like these. Scientists have worked out what they looked like from their fossils. Trilobites died out millions of years ago, but sponges, sea lilies and jellyfish still live in the sea.

Fossils of plants and animals which lived together at the same time are found in the same place in the rock. Scientists can tell what the weather was like by looking at the kind of plants that grew. Here is what they think life in the sea looked like, about 550 million years ago.

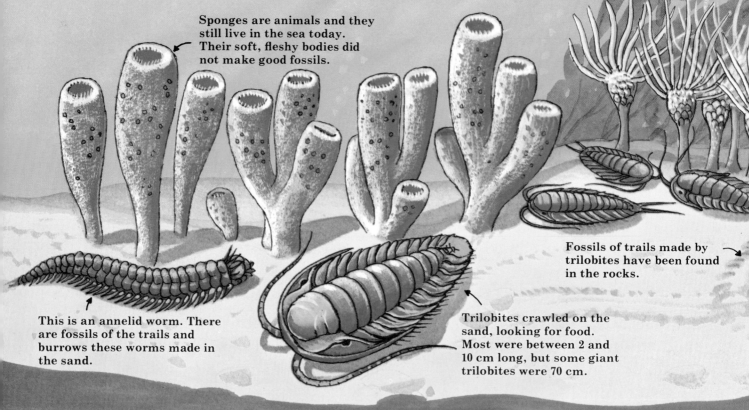

Sponges are animals and they still live in the sea today. Their soft, fleshy bodies did not make good fossils.

Fossils of trails made by trilobites have been found in the rocks.

This is an annelid worm. There are fossils of the trails and burrows these worms made in the sand.

Trilobites crawled on the sand, looking for food. Most were between 2 and 10 cm long, but some giant trilobites were 70 cm.

Reading rocks

Fossils are the same age as the sedimentary rock in which they are found. Scientists can work out how old the rocks are, so they know the age of the fossils too.

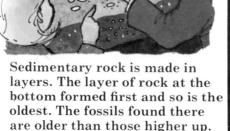

Sedimentary rock is made in layers. The layer of rock at the bottom formed first and so is the oldest. The fossils found there are older than those higher up.

1 Make some trilobites

CUT OUT OVAL SHAPE

To make a model trilobite, roll out a piece of plasticine. Then cut a flat pear-shaped piece for the trilobite's body.

There were no plants or animals on the bare rocky land.

Jellyfish like these still live in the sea and catch food with their tentacles.

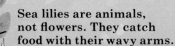

Sea lilies are animals, not flowers. They catch food with their wavy arms.

These are called lamp shells because they look like a kind of ancient Roman lamp.

The name trilobite means "three-lobed" and describes the shape of its body.

1 Fossil trilobites

Trilobites made good fossils because they had hard skin. Their antennae did not become fossils, but marks show where they joined the body.

Fossil jellyfish

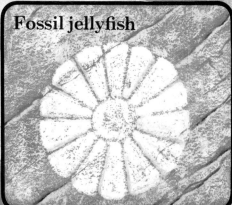

Jellyfish did not make good fossils because their bodies were too soft. This one left a print of the shape of its body in soft mud.

2

The trilobite's hard skin protected it from danger. Some trilobites could curl into a tight ball to protect themselves.

2

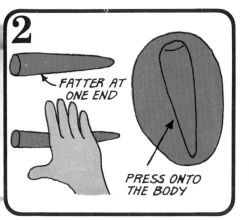

FATTER AT ONE END

PRESS ONTO THE BODY

Next, roll a sausage of plasticine the same length as the oval. One end should be a bit fatter than the other. Press this along the centre of the body.

3

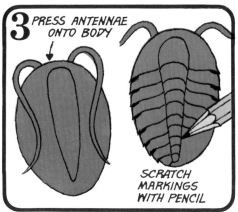

PRESS ANTENNAE ONTO BODY

SCRATCH MARKINGS WITH PENCIL

Roll a long, thin sausage shape and cut it in half to make two antennae. Then scratch the markings on the trilobite with the point of a pencil.

4

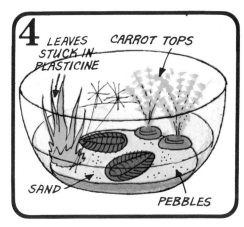

LEAVES STUCK IN PLASTICINE

CARROT TOPS

SAND

PEBBLES

You could make an underwater scene by putting the trilobites on some sand in a bowl. To make plants cut off the tops of carrots and put them in water to sprout.

The First Fish

For millions of years the seas stayed warm and calm. Trilobites still crawled over the sea floor, but there were new creatures too. Some had shells and others lived in a chalky skeleton of coral. All these animals are called invertebrates because they had no backbones.

As time passed, some animals developed backbones and became fish. Animals with backbones are called vertebrates. The way animals slowly change, is called evolution. This is explained on page 13.

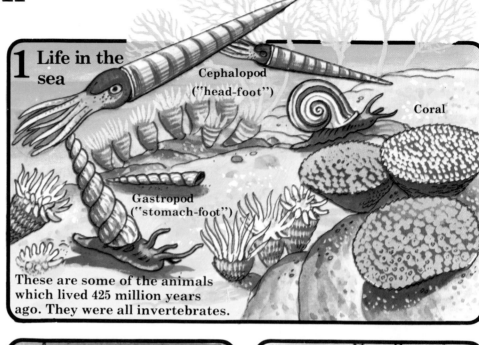

1 Life in the sea

Cephalopod ("head-foot")

Gastropod ("stomach-foot")

Coral

These are some of the animals which lived 425 million years ago. They were all invertebrates.

2 about 1 m long

The first animals with backbones were fish-like creatures called ostracoderms. They had thick, armoured skin and their name means "shell-skinned".

3 *Acanthodii* fish, about 10 cm long

The first fish were jawless but later fish had jaws with sharp teeth. They could swim very fast to catch other sea creatures and eat them.

Plants on land

Plants first grew on the land 400 million years ago. They grew on wet, marshy ground near water. Then stronger plants grew and spread over the rest of the land.

The great drought

About 375 million years ago the weather became very hot. There were long seasons of drought and the lakes and rivers dried up in the hot sun.

Many fish died as the lakes shrank. Their bodies lay on the sun-baked mud and sand blew over them. It was so dry that their bodies did not rot away.

Fossil fish

This is the fossil of a group of fish which died when the lakes dried up. Their bodies were so well preserved that the fossils show the shape of their scales.

Prehistoric sea monster

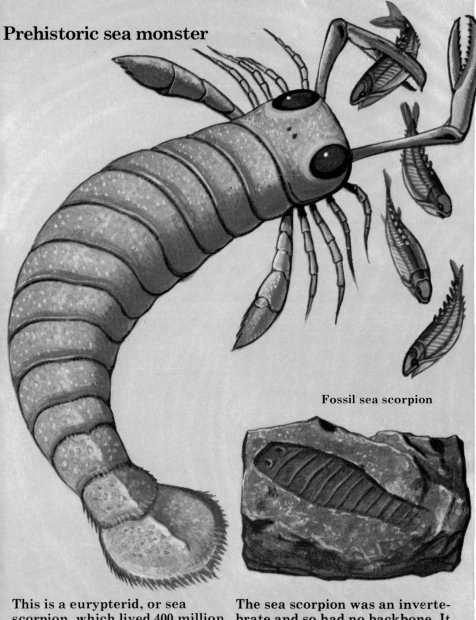

Fossil sea scorpion

This is a eurypterid, or sea scorpion, which lived 400 million years ago. It was about 3 m long and caught small creatures with its long pincers.

The sea scorpion was an invertebrate and so had no backbone. It had a hard skin which was jointed so that it could move. On this fossil you can see the marks of its eyes.

Fish on land

This is a fish called *Eusthenopteron*. It survived the drought because it was able to drag itself across the land to find a pool or stream. It was about 50 cm long.

Eusthenopteron had a lung as well as gills, so it could breathe on land. It had strong bones in its fins which it used to pull itself along the ground.

Make a sea scorpion

Here is how to make a wriggly cardboard model of a sea scorpion.

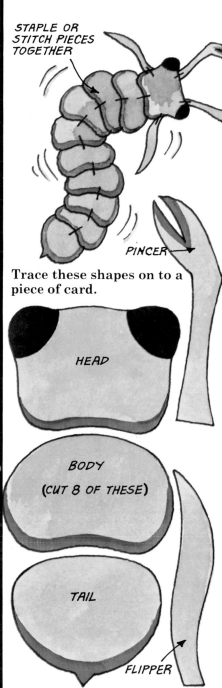

STAPLE OR STITCH PIECES TOGETHER

PINCER

Trace these shapes on to a piece of card.

HEAD

BODY (CUT 8 OF THESE)

TAIL

FLIPPER

Paint the shapes and then cut them out of the card. Take one of the body pieces and staple or stitch it to the head. Then join on the rest of the pieces and put the tail on the end. Staple the flippers to the side of the head and put the pincers on the front. To make the scorpion wriggle, twitch its tail.

Animals Crawl on to Land

The first creatures to survive on land were fish with lungs and strong fins. Over the next few million years they slowly changed and became more suited to living on the land. Their fins became legs which were strong enough for walking and their lungs grew bigger.

Animals which live on land but have to return to the water to lay their eggs are called amphibians. The first land animals on Earth were amphibians. The weather was hot and rainy then and there were plenty of pools where they could lay their eggs.

The first amphibian

One of the first amphibians was *Ichthyostega*. It was about 1 m long and lived 345 million years ago. It had strong legs and feet with five toes, but its tail was like that of a fish.

Its legs were strong enough to carry it on land, but it probably stayed most of the time in the water, swimming and catching fish to eat.

Did you know?

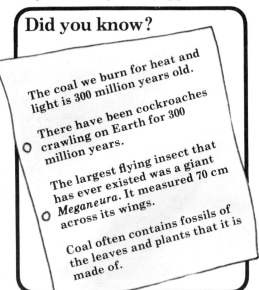

- The coal we burn for heat and light is 300 million years old.

- There have been cockroaches crawling on Earth for 300 million years.

- The largest flying insect that has ever existed was a giant *Meganeura*. It measured 70 cm across its wings.

- Coal often contains fossils of the leaves and plants that it is made of.

Insects

Meganeura

The first insects lived at this time too. This is the fossil of *Meganeura*, an insect which looked like a huge dragonfly. It lived near swamps and ate other insects.

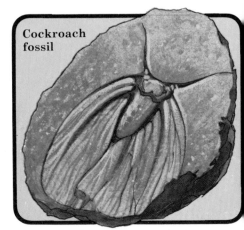

Cockroach fossil

This is the fossil of a cockroach which lived at the same time as the amphibians. Cockroaches, and other insects were probably eaten by the amphibians.

The life of amphibians

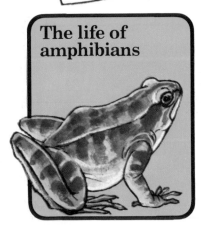

The modern frog is an amphibian. The adult frog lives on land and its life-cycle is the same as that of the first amphibians.

Frogs have to lay their eggs in water. The eggs have no shells and would dry up if they were laid on the land.

The eggs hatch into tadpoles which swim in the water with their tails. They breathe through gills and eat plants.

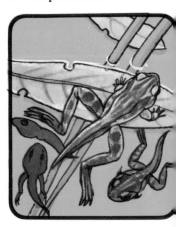

As the tadpoles grow, the tails and gills disappear. They grow into adult frog with legs and lungs and move onto the land.

Prehistoric forests

Thick forests covered the land about 300 million years ago. In the forests there were lakes and swamps full of rotting leaves and plants.

Giant clubmosses grew 30 m tall with trunks nearly a metre across. Scars on the trunks were left by leaves which had dropped off.

Meganeura

This is the trunk of *Calamites*, a kind of horsetail which grew 18 m tall.

Amphibians lived near lakes and swamps in the forest and ate fish or insects.

Cockroaches ate the leaves and rotting plants.

Horsetails like these still grow in marshy places today.

Mosses, ferns and liverworts grew on the wet ground.

1 How coal is made

Coal is made from plants which grew 300 million years ago. Dead branches and leaves fell into the swamps. Slowly they built up into a thick layer of rotting plants.

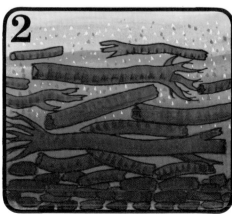

2

Later the swamps were covered by the sea. The rotting wood and leaves were buried under thick layers of mud and sand at the bottom of the sea.

3

The heavy layers of sand and mud squashed the plants and changed them into coal. Now we dig through the ground to reach the coal and burn it to make heat.

11

The First Reptiles

About 280 million years ago the weather changed again and became very hot and dry. The swamps slowly dried up and most of the amphibians died.

Now a new kind of animal evolved. It had thick, scaly skin and laid eggs which were protected by a leathery shell. This type of animal is called a reptile.

The new reptiles laid their eggs in the warm sand or in nests of rotting plants. The shell protected them from drying up in the hot sun.

Diadectes was one of the earliest reptiles. It measured about 2 m from its nose to the end of its long tail. Fossils of its teeth show that it ate plants.

Its legs stuck out on either side of its body and so did not support it very well. But they were strong enough to lift its body off the ground and take quite long steps.

Land animals of 200 million years ago

Gradually, over millions of years, some of the reptiles changed. They had different teeth, their legs were stronger and some of them had hair instead of scales. Animals which have hair and suckle their young are called mammals. Parts of some of the reptiles' bodies were like mammals and these are called mammal-like reptiles.

Lystrosaurus was a mammal-like reptile, which lived in swamps and ate plants. It was about 1½ m long.

Sauroctonus was a fierce mammal-like reptile. It had long, sharp teeth and ate other animals.

Euparkeria was a reptile which lived about 225 million years ago. It was about 1 m long and was the ancestor of some of the dinosaurs.

Thrinaxodon was a mammal-like reptile which had developed hair, but it probably still laid eggs. It was about the size of a cat.

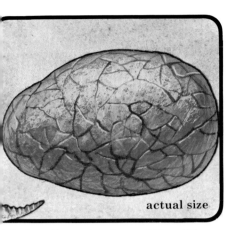

actual size

his fossil egg is about 225 million ears old. We do not know which eptile laid it but we can see that he tough shell dried and cracked efore it became a fossil.

Edaphosaurus was a reptile which lived 250 million years ago. It was about 3 m long. The strange sail on its back was made of long bones covered with skin.

It may have used the sail to keep its body at the right temperature. When it was cold it heated up quickly by turning the sail to the heat of the sun.

What is a reptile?

Reptiles are animals which have scaly skin and lay eggs with shells. They are cold-blooded, which means they cannot control the temperature of their body.

What is evolution?

The way animals slowly change, over millions of years, and become new kinds of animals, is called evolution. The first person to discover how animals evolve was a scientist called Charles Darwin, who lived over a hundred years ago.

Darwin showed that no two animals are exactly the same, even among the same type of animal. Some of them are taller, or stronger, or have other features which may

make them more suited to living in their surroundings.

The animals which are better adapted survive to become adults and have babies like themselves. Eventually, after many generations of babies, the animals which are less well adapted have all died out. This is called the "survival of the fittest" and it explains how a group of animals evolves and becomes well suited to its surroundings.

1

About 375 million years ago the weather changed and there were long, dry seasons. One kind of fish, called *Eusthenopteron*, was

2

able to survive because it had strong fins and could drag itself across the land to find pools. Many of the other fish died.

3

Over the next few million years, some of the descendants of *Eusthenopteron* were born with even stronger fins.

4

Eventually, about 345 million years ago, some animals had legs and these were the first amphibians.

The Age of Dinosaurs

Dinosaurs were a group of reptiles which lived from 200 million years to 65 million years ago. Palaeontologists have found thousands of fossils which show what dinosaurs looked like and how they lived. There are fossils of bones and teeth, footprints and skin and even fossil eggs with baby dinosaurs inside.

The name dinosaur means "terrible lizard". There were dinosaurs on the Earth for about 135 million years, which is 70 times longer than people have existed.

The first dinosaurs

These are two of the earliest dinosaurs. *Fabrosaurus* was about 1 m long. It ate plants and usually walked on four legs, but could run faster on two.

The other dinosaur, *Coelophysis* was about 2 m long. It walked on two legs and had a long tail to help it balance. It had sharp teeth and ate meat.

Dinosaur timetable

There were lots of different kinds of dinosaurs, but they did not all live at the same time. This chart shows you when some of the main kinds of dinosaurs lived.

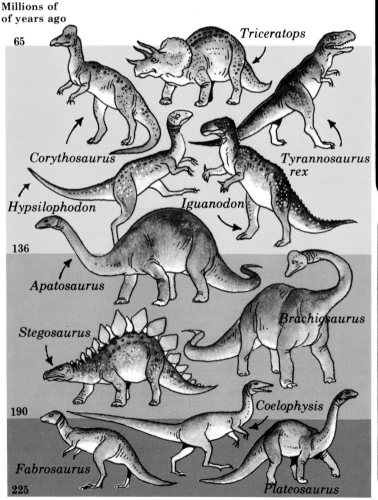

Millions of of years ago

Prehistoric footprints

Fossil footprints of *Megalosaurus*, a huge meat-eating dinosaur, show the shape of its three toes. The footprints were made when it walked on soft mud. The mud was baked by the sun and later covered by sand. This hardened to form rock which still had the shape of the footprints in it.

Fossil skin

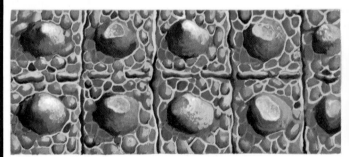

This is a piece of fossil skin from the dinosaur *Scolosaurus*. This dinosaur had thick, scaly skin with spikes to protect it.

You can see the shape of the scales and the bony spikes. The fossil is stone-coloured and does not show the real colour of the skin.

Dinosaurs' ancestors

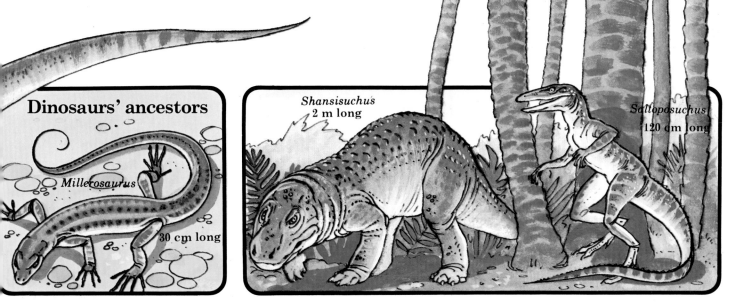

Millerosaurus
30 cm long

Shansisuchus
2 m long

Saltoposuchus
120 cm long

The ancestors of the dinosaurs were reptiles like *Millerosaurus* which lived 250 million years ago. They crawled on the ground with their legs stuck out at their sides.

Shansisuchus was a reptile which lived 225 million years ago. Its legs were tucked under its body and lifted it well off the ground, although it was a heavy animal.

Saltoposuchus was the ancestor of some of the two-legged dinosaurs. Dinosaurs had stronger legs than the early reptiles and had long tails to help them balance.

Baby dinosaurs

Baby dinosaurs hatched from eggs which the mother dinosaur laid in the sand.

Fossil eggs of the dinosaur *Protoceratops* have been found with the bones of the baby dinosaurs inside. The young looked just like the adult dinosaurs. *Protoceratops* was a ceratopsian dinosaur, about 2 m long.

The mother *Protoceratops* dug a nest in the sand and laid her eggs in it. But she did not look after them. Eggs were sometimes buried in sand and the babies died.

Monster quiz

We have mixed up the letters in these reptiles' names. Can you work out what the names ought to be be? The answers are on the last page of this book.

1 Donoguani—This one had spikes on its thumbs.

2 Pertosaurs—These were flying reptiles.

3 Gosetsaurus—This dinosaur had spikes on its tail.

4 Rantynosaurus—A very fierce dinosaur.

5 Chabriosaurus—The biggest and heaviest dinosaur.

6 Harodsaurs—These dinosaurs had bony crests on their heads.

Finding Dinosaur Fossils

Fossils form in sedimentary rocks, so palaeontologists know where to look for them. When they go to a place where there are sedimentary rocks they will probably find fossils.

The most exciting thing to find is a dinosaur fossil. It may be a dinosaur that is already known, but they might find a new kind of dinosaur that no-one has found before.

Once they have found the fossil bones it may take several years to put them together and work out what the dinosaur looked like.

If the skeleton has fallen apart, the palaeontologists note where each bone is lying. This helps them when they try to put the skeleton together again.

The fossil bones are very fragile. They have to be wrapped in wet tissue and then covered with strips of cloth dipped in plaster of Paris to protect them.

Making mistakes

Sometimes scientists make mistakes when they reconstruct dinosaurs. When they first discovered *Iguanodon*, they thought it had a horn on its nose.

Later they realised that *Iguanodon* had no horn but a spike on each of its thumbs. Now scientists know more about dinosaurs and make fewer mistakes.

Fossil skeleton

The picture below shows the fossil skeleton of the dinosaur *Plateosaurus*. On the right you can see what palaeontologists think *Plateosaurus* looked like when it was alive.

In museums, you can sometimes see wires holding the skeleton in a life-like pose. If it is a very rare fossil, fibre-glass models of the bones are shown instead of the real fossil bones.

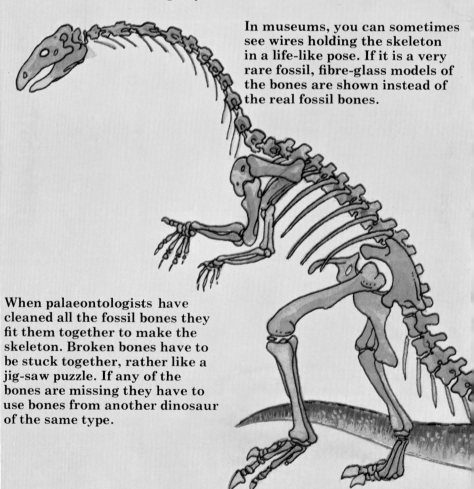

When palaeontologists have cleaned all the fossil bones they fit them together to make the skeleton. Broken bones have to be stuck together, rather like a jig-saw puzzle. If any of the bones are missing they have to use bones from another dinosaur of the same type.

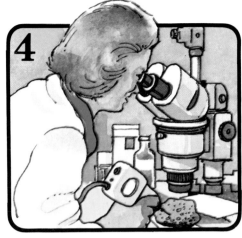

Sometimes the fossil is almost completely buried in solid rock. Then the whole block of rock has to be cut out and taken back to the laboratory.

The rock round the fossil is removed with tiny drills, or washed away with chemicals. The palaeontologist has to be very careful not to damage the fossil.

The living dinosaur

Plateosaurus ("flat lizard") was about 6 m long. It was one of the first plant-eating dinosaurs and lived about 200 million years ago.

Clues on the fossil bones help palaeontologists reconstruct what a living dinosaur looked like. All animals' bones have lumps and scars which show where the muscles joined them. By studying the lumps on the fossil bones, scientists can work out the shape of the dinosaur's muscles.

Fossils of dinosaur skin show that they had thick, scaly skin, like a modern crocodile's. There are no fossils to show us what colour they were. Many large, modern reptiles are greeny-brown, so perhaps dinosaurs were the same.

Pipecleanosaurus

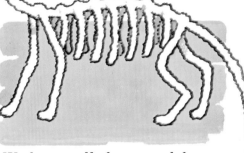

We have called our model dinosaur Pipecleanosaurus because it is made of pipe-cleaners.

To make Pipecleanosaurus, join two pipe-cleaners by twisting the ends together. Then bend them to make the curve of the dinosaur's spine.

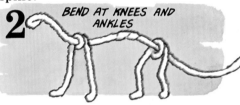

Bend two pipe-cleaners in half for the legs. Twist them round the spine as shown in the picture. Then bend them at the knees and ankles.

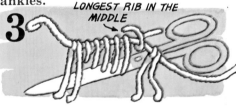

To make ribs, cut one piece of pipe-cleaner 8 cm long, two 7 cm, two 6 cm and two 5 cm long. Then twist them round the spine.

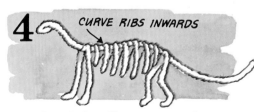

Now bend the ribs to curve them inwards slightly. You could make models of other skeletons in this book too.

What Dinosaurs Ate

Some dinosaurs ate plants and others were meat-eaters. The giant dinosaurs, such as *Brachiosaurus*, ate only plants and must have eaten nearly a tonne of leaves every day to stay alive. Animals which eat plants are called herbivores and meat-eating animals are called carnivores.

Carnivorous dinosaurs had long, sharp claws for attacking their prey and pointed teeth for tearing the meat. The herbivores had to defend themselves from the fierce carnivores.

Plant-eating dinosaurs

Camarasaurus

Scolosaurus ("thorn lizard") about 6 m long

The herbivores were not all competing for the same food. The giant dinosaurs could reach the leaves in the treetops and small dinosaurs ate plants on the ground.

Fighting off the meat-eaters

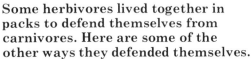

Some herbivores lived together in packs to defend themselves from carnivores. Here are some of the other ways they defended themselves.

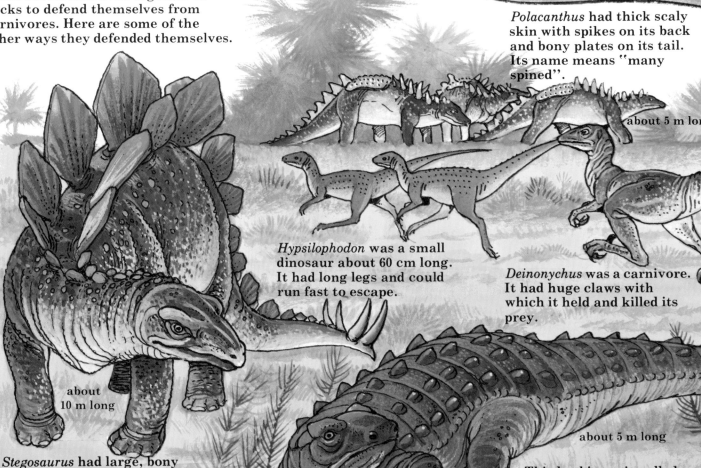

Polacanthus had thick scaly skin with spikes on its back and bony plates on its tail. Its name means "many spined".

about 5 m long

Hypsilophodon was a small dinosaur about 60 cm long. It had long legs and could run fast to escape.

Deinonychus was a carnivore. It had huge claws with which it held and killed its prey.

about 10 m long

Stegosaurus had large, bony plates growing from the skin on its back and spikes like daggers on its tail. Its plates are like roof tiles and its name means "roof-lizard".

about 5 m long

This herbivore is called *Euoplocephalus*. It stunned its attackers with the bony club on its tail. It measured 5 m from nose to tail.

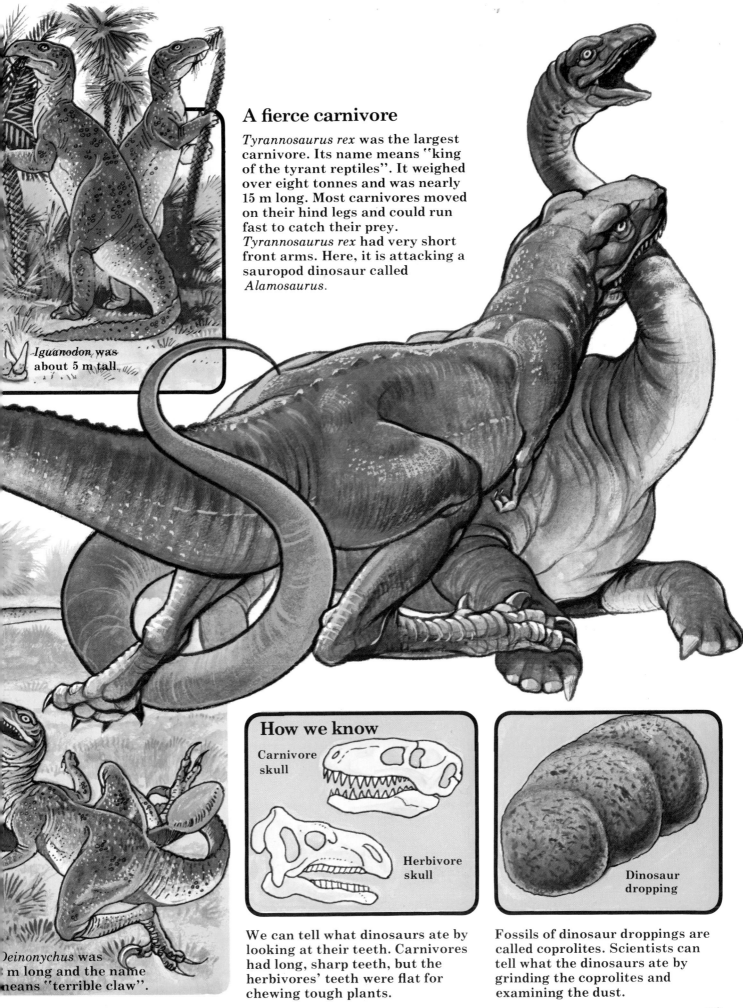

Iguanodon was
about 5 m tall.

A fierce carnivore

Tyrannosaurus rex was the largest carnivore. Its name means "king of the tyrant reptiles". It weighed over eight tonnes and was nearly 15 m long. Most carnivores moved on their hind legs and could run fast to catch their prey. *Tyrannosaurus rex* had very short front arms. Here, it is attacking a sauropod dinosaur called *Alamosaurus*.

Deinonychus was
m long and the name
means "terrible claw".

How we know

Carnivore skull

Herbivore skull

Dinosaur dropping

We can tell what dinosaurs ate by looking at their teeth. Carnivores had long, sharp teeth, but the herbivores' teeth were flat for chewing tough plants.

Fossils of dinosaur droppings are called coprolites. Scientists can tell what the dinosaurs ate by grinding the coprolites and examining the dust.

The Giant Dinosaurs

The giant dinosaurs are the largest land animals that have ever lived. They ate only plants and spent much of the time in swamps, where they were safe from the meat-eating dinosaurs. They belong to a group called the sauropod dinosaurs.

The heaviest dinosaur

Brachiosaurus is the largest dinosaur that has ever been discovered. It was 25 m long, 12 m high and must have weighed about 81 tonnes. It had a very long neck and could reach for leaves in the top of trees. Its name means "arm-lizard".

1 How they moved

These dinosaurs lived in swamps. It was easier for them to move in the water than on dry land.

2

They had thick, pillar-like legs to support the weight of their huge bodies.

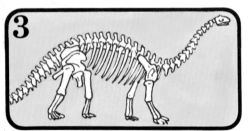

3

The bones in their legs were very strong, but their spines were hollow to make them lighter.

4

In deep water they pushed themselves along with their front legs and steered with their tails.

In herds for safety

Apatosaurus used to be called Brontosaurus. These dinosaurs stayed together in herds to protect themselves from attack by the meat-eating dinosaurs.

The longest dinosaur

Diplodocus measured 28 m from its nose to the tip of its tail. It lived in the swamps and came on land to eat plants and leaves and to lay its eggs.

The brain of *Diplodocus* was no bigger than a hen's egg. It had another nerve centre between its legs which controlled its back legs and tail.

Nostril

The sauropod dinosaurs all had very small heads. Their nostrils were on top of their heads so they could breathe when they were swimming.

Why were they so big?

Dinosaurs were probably cold-blooded. This means that their body temperature was controlled by the heat of the sun. If the weather was cool, the dinosaurs

got cold. But some of the dinosaurs were so big that it took them a very long time to cool. Their great size kept them warm and this was probably one of the reasons they were so big.

Measure some dinosaurs

1 METRE

To see how big some of the dinosaurs were, pace out their lengths in a park or play-ground. Your pace is probably about 1 m long. (If you want to be exact you can measure it.) To measure *Diplodocus*, which was 28 m long, mark where you start and take 28 paces. Then look back and see just how huge it really was.

Apatosaurus means "deceptive lizard". It was about 18 m long, nearly as long as a railway carriage, and weighed about 30 tonnes. Compared to the size of its body, it had a smaller brain than any other animal.

Smallest dinosaur

Compsognathus was the smallest dinosaur. It was about the size of a crow. It fed on insects and small reptiles and could run very fast.

Horned and Crested Dinosaurs

Some dinosaurs had strange crests of bone on their heads. These belonged to a group called the hadrosaurs. The crest probably worked as a very sensitive nose which helped the hadrosaurs smell enemies from far away.

Another group of dinosaurs had horns on their heads and bony shields round their necks. These were the ceratopsians.

Hadrosaurs and ceratopsians were plant-eating dinosaurs. They probably developed their special heads to protect them from the carnivores.

Duck-billed dinosaurs

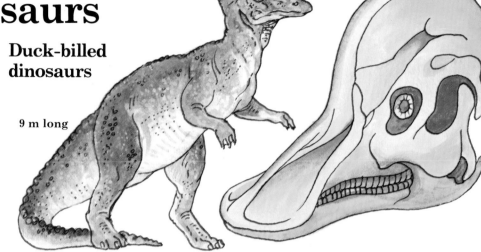

9 m long

Corythosaurus was a hadrosaur with a crest shaped like a helmet. The crest was made of bone with air tubes inside which led to the animal's lungs.

The hadrosaurs are also called duck-billed dinosaurs, because their jaws ended in a horny, toothless beak. They used this to clip leaves from the trees.

Horned dinosaurs

11 m long

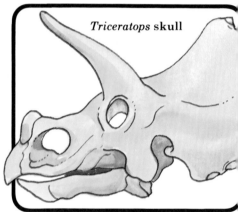

Triceratops skull

Triceratops was one of the ceratopsian dinosaurs. It had three horns, one on its nose and one over each eye. Round its neck it had a long shield of bone.

At the end of its mouth it had a beak to chop through the stems of plants. It ate very tough leaves and had special teeth with flat surfaces to chew through them.

This is the skull of *Triceratops*. Ceratopsian dinosaurs had strong jaw muscles to help them chew tough plants. The bony neck shield supported these jaw muscles.

Bone-heads

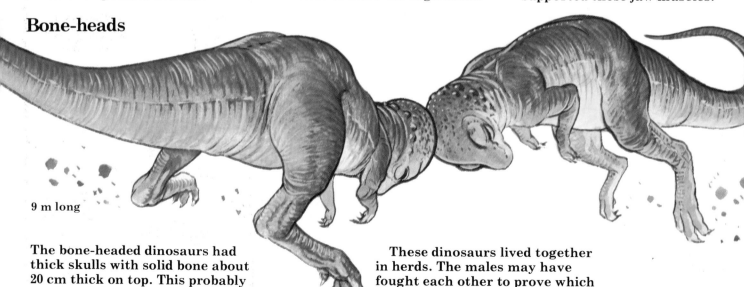

9 m long

The bone-headed dinosaurs had thick skulls with solid bone about 20 cm thick on top. This probably protected them when they fought.

These dinosaurs lived together in herds. The males may have fought each other to prove which of them was the strongest.

Parasaurolophus had the longest crest of all the hadrosaurs. It measured 2 m from the tip of its nose. Hadrosaurs probably lived some of the time in water. Their hands were webbed like a duck's feet and their feet had hoofs.

about 12 m long

Hadrosaur teeth

Hadrosaurs had rows of hundreds of small, sharp teeth in their jaws. They ate tough pine needles and when their teeth wore down, new ones grew to replace them.

Shadow monsters

Can you recognise these reptiles from their shadows? They are all shown in this book, so look through the pages if you get stuck.

1
2
3
4
5
6
7
8
9
10
11

(Answers on the last page of this book)

Sea Monsters

At the same time as dinosaurs lived there were huge creatures living in the sea. They evolved from reptiles which lived on the land 280 million years ago. Over millions of years their bodies became smooth and streamlined to suit their life in the sea and their legs became flippers.

These sea creatures were reptiles, but they did not lay eggs. There are fossils of sea reptiles with babies inside them and these show that they gave birth to live young. This picture shows three different kinds of sea reptile.

A famous fossil find

Mary Anning lived in Dorset about 150 years ago, in a small village by the sea. She used to go fossil hunting along the beach with her father.

They found lots of fossils of ammonites and when she was 11 she found a nearly perfect fossil of an ichthyosaur.

She was the first person to discover a complete plesiosaur fossil. Her fossils are now in the Natural History Museum, London.

Ichthyosaurs were very fast swimmers. They had strong tail fins and could probably leap out of the water. Their long jaws were full of sharp teeth and they ate fish and shellfish. There were lots of different kinds of ichthyosaur which means "fish lizard" and some were about 12 m long.

Pliosaurs had short necks and large heads with lots of sharp teeth. They had strong flippers and could dive deep into the water to catch fish and ammonites.

Fossil ichthyosaur

This fossil of an ichthyosaur is so well preserved that we can see the outline of its skin. It had very large eyes so that it could see in the dark water.

It used its strong tail fin for swimming and steered with the fins on its sides. The fin on its back stopped its body rolling from side to side as it swam.

Fossil teeth marks

This is the fossil shell of an ammonite, a sea creature which lived at the same time as the sea reptiles. This one has marks of a sea reptile's teeth on it.

Plesiosaurs had very long necks. They pulled themselves through the water with large, flat flippers and could swing their heads from side to side looking for fish. Some were about 12 m long.

Plesiosaur skeleton

This is a model of the fossil skeleton of a plesiosaur. These sea reptiles had small skulls and some of them had as many as 76 bones in their long necks.

The plesiosaurs and other sea reptiles evolved from land animals. Their leg bones changed shape and became paddles for swimming in the water.

Felt pliosaur

You will need some felt, dried lentils or rice, tracing paper and two small buttons.

1 Fold the tracing paper. Put the fold on the edge of the pattern and trace it.

2 Keep the paper folded and cut out the tracing. Then unfold it and pin it to the felt.

3 Cut out two of these shapes in felt and pin them together.

← PUT FOLDED EDGE OF TRACING PAPER ON THIS LINE

4 Stitch round the edge of the felt leaving an opening between the flippers.

5 Pour the lentils or rice into the pliosaur and then sew up the hole.

SEW ON BUTTONS FOR EYES

Flying Reptiles

The flying reptiles are called pterosaurs. They lived at the same time as the dinosaurs. Some scientists think they were not reptiles, but were warm-blooded and furry.

The pterosaurs were not very strong fliers. Their wings were made of leathery skin supported by their fourth finger which had grown very long. They probably glided with outstretched wings and swooped down to catch fish or insects. If they were in danger, they could escape into the air, out of reach of the dinosaurs.

Dimorphodon lived about 190 million years ago and was one of the first pterosaurs. It measured nearly 2 m across its wings and had a long tail.

Like the other pterosaurs it had claws on its wings and large back claws. Its head was large and clumsy and it had sharp teeth in its beak-like jaws.

Toothless gliders

Pteranodon was one of the largest flying reptiles. It measured 8 m across its wings, but only weighed about 20 kg. Its claws were not very strong and it probably found it difficult to move on land.

It had a long, bony crest on the back of its head and a pointed beak with no teeth. It may have soared over the sea, looking for fish which it caught in its beak-like jaws and fed to its young.

Fossil pterosaur

This is the fossil skeleton of *Pterodactylus*, one of the smallest pterosaurs. It shows the bones of the long fourth finger which supported the wing. You can see the teeth in its beak too. Its head was flat on top with not much space for the brain.

Pterodactylus was about the size of a starling. These pterosaurs lived together in flocks and probably slept hanging upside-down in trees or caves. They lived near the sea and ate insects, which they probably snapped up in their jaws as they flew.

Rhamphorhynchus

Rhamphorhynchus measured about 2 m across the wings and had a long neck and head. Its tail ended in a diamond-shaped flap of skin which acted as a rudder and helped it to steer.

The bones of *Rhamphorhynchus* and other pterosaurs were hollow and filled with air. This made them light so they could glide more easily. Pterosaurs laid eggs but no nests have yet been found.

New Discoveries

A fossil of the largest flying creature that has ever existed was found in 1975, in Texas, U.S.A. It was a pterosaur with a wing-span of about 12 m, which is larger than a two-seater aeroplane. This pterosaur has been named *Quetzalcoatlus*. It probably lived inland and fed on dead animals, like vultures do today.

Hairy pterosaur

Sometimes palaeontologists find fossils which change all their ideas about an animal. In 1966, in the U.S.S.R., they found the fossil of a pterosaur which looks as though it was covered with fluffy hair. It has been named *Sordes pilosus*.

Some scientists do not agree that the fossil shows hair. They think it may have been something like hair which kept the pterosaurs warm, or helped them to fly.

27

The First Bird

All the birds which live now are descended from the dinosaurs. The first bird is called *Archaeopteryx* and it lived 150 million years ago. *Archaeopteryx* developed from small dinosaurs like *Compsognathus*. Its skeleton was still like a reptile's but fossils show that it had feathers and so it was a true bird.

   Archaeopteryx was about the size of a crow. It lived in woodlands and ate berries and insects. It could not fly very well and probably climbed trees and then glided down to the ground again.

Archaeopteryx had strong claws with one toe pointing backwards. This helped it to grip branches and perch in trees. Its long tail kept it steady as it flew down from the trees.

Feathered fossil

It probably found it difficult to take off from the ground as it was quite heavy. It climbed up trees, clinging to the bark with the long claws on its wings.

This fossil of *Archaeopteryx* shows the feathers on the wings and tail very clearly. It had teeth in its jaw like a reptile, and a long bony tail. Like modern birds, it had hollow bones to make it lighter. The name *Archaeopteryx* means "ancient wing".

Scaly head

Archaeopteryx's head was covered with scaly skin like the dinosaurs'. On the rest of its body the scales had become feathers.

28

The End of the Dinosaurs

About 65 million years ago, the dinosaurs became extinct. All the pterosaurs and the sea reptiles died out too. Palaeontologists do not know exactly why but they think perhaps these animals could not adapt to changes which were taking place on the Earth.

When dinosaurs were alive the weather was warm all the year round. About 65 million years ago, it became cooler with cold winters. At the same time, great movements in the earth crumpled the rocks and made high mountains.

Dinosaurs were cold-blooded and needed the sun to keep them warm. When their huge bodies got very cold it took too long for them to warm up again and many died.

There were probably other reasons too why dinosaurs died out. But now scientists have only the fossils in the rocks from which to find out why they became extinct.

The survivors

Tuatara lizards lived at the same time as the dinosaurs. But they did not become extinct. There are very few tuatara lizards living now and they may soon become extinct.

This is a mammal called *Protictis* which lived about 60 million years ago. Mammals are warm-blooded and they survived when the dinosaurs died out.

Great Tit

Mistle Thrush

Bullfinch

The birds that live today are the true descendants of the dinosaurs. They evolved from the first bird, *Archaeopteryx*, which developed from a small kind of dinosaur.

Living reptiles

Many different kinds of reptiles live today. Many of them are threatened with extinction because people kill them for their beautiful skins.

Tortoise

Snake

Lizard

Crocodile

Time Chart

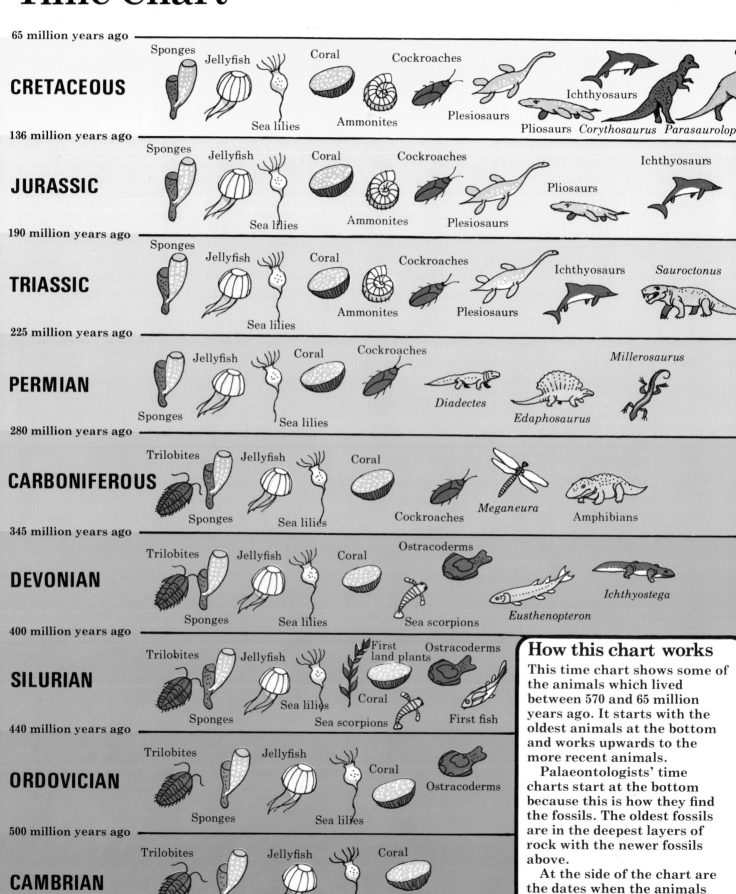

65 million years ago

CRETACEOUS

Sponges Jellyfish Coral Cockroaches Sea lilies Ammonites Plesiosaurs Ichthyosaurs Pliosaurs *Corythosaurus* *Parasaurolop*

136 million years ago

JURASSIC

Sponges Jellyfish Coral Cockroaches Sea lilies Ammonites Plesiosaurs Pliosaurs Ichthyosaurs

190 million years ago

TRIASSIC

Sponges Jellyfish Coral Cockroaches Sea lilies Ammonites Plesiosaurs Ichthyosaurs *Sauroctonus*

225 million years ago

PERMIAN

Jellyfish Coral Cockroaches *Millerosaurus* Sponges Sea lilies *Diadectes* *Edaphosaurus*

280 million years ago

CARBONIFEROUS

Trilobites Jellyfish Coral Sponges Sea lilies Cockroaches *Meganeura* Amphibians

345 million years ago

DEVONIAN

Trilobites Jellyfish Coral Ostracoderms Sponges Sea lilies Sea scorpions *Eusthenopteron* *Ichthyostega*

400 million years ago

SILURIAN

Trilobites Jellyfish First land plants Ostracoderms Sponges Coral Sea lilies Sea scorpions First fish

440 million years ago

ORDOVICIAN

Trilobites Jellyfish Coral Sponges Ostracoderms Sea lilies

500 million years ago

CAMBRIAN

Trilobites Jellyfish Coral Sponges Sea lilies

570 million years ago

How this chart works

This time chart shows some of the animals which lived between 570 and 65 million years ago. It starts with the oldest animals at the bottom and works upwards to the more recent animals.

   Palaeontologists' time charts start at the bottom because this is how they find the fossils. The oldest fossils are in the deepest layers of rock with the newer fossils above.

   At the side of the chart are the dates when the animals lived and the names of the different periods of prehistory.

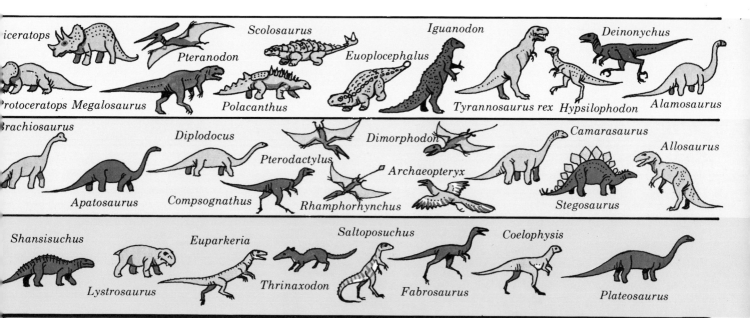

iceratops *Pteranodon* *Scolosaurus* *Iguanodon* *Deinonychus* *Euoplocephalus* *rotoceratops* *Megalosaurus* *Polacanthus* *Tyrannosaurus rex* *Hypsilophodon* *Alamosaurus* *Brachiosaurus* *Diplodocus* *Dimorphodon* *Camarasaurus* *Allosaurus* *Pterodactylus* *Archaeopteryx* *Apatosaurus* *Compsognathus* *Rhamphorhynchus* *Stegosaurus* *Shansisuchus* *Euparkeria* *Saltoposuchus* *Coelophysis* *Lystrosaurus* *Thrinaxodon* *Fabrosaurus* *Plateosaurus*

Prehistory Words

Ammonites
Sea creatures with coiled shells which lived 150 million years ago.

Amphibians
Animals, such as frogs, which live on land and lay their eggs in water.

Carnivores
Animals which eat meat.

Ceratopsians
Dinosaurs with horns and shields of bone round their necks.

Coprolite
Fossil animal dropping.

Dinosaurs
A group of reptiles which lived from 200 million to 65 million years ago.

Evolution
The way animals slowly change over a very long time and become different animals.

Fossils
Remains of ancient plants and animals preserved in the rocks.

Hadrosaurs
A group of dinosaurs, most of which had crests on their heads.

Herbivores
Animals which eat plants.

Ichthyosaurs
Swimming reptiles with fish-shaped bodies.

Invertebrates
Animals which do not have backbones.

Mammals
Animals which have fur, give birth to babies and can control their own body temperature.

Mammal-like reptiles
Reptiles which have some parts of their body like a mammal.

Ostracoderms
Fish-like sea creatures with thick, armoured skin which lived 400 million years ago.

Palaeontologist
A scientist who studies fossils to find out about prehistoric plants and animals.

Palaeontology
The study of prehistoric plants and animals.

Plesiosaurs
Reptiles with long necks which swim with four paddle-like legs.

Pliosaurs
Reptiles with short necks which swim with four paddle-like legs.

Pterosaurs
Flying reptiles with wings made of skin.

Reptiles
Animals which have scaly skin, lay eggs and cannot control their body temperature.

Sauropods
Very large, four-legged, herbivorous dinosaurs.

Sedimentary rock
Rock made from sand and mud which have been pressed down very hard and changed to rock.

Trilobites
Sea creatures with hard skin which lived 550 million years ago.

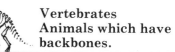

Vertebrates
Animals which have backbones.

Mammals Take Over

For millions of years, while the great, scaly-skinned dinosaurs were alive, small furry creatures lived in the woods and undergrowth. They probably came out at night when the dinosaurs were asleep and ate insects, lizards and plants.

These creatures were the first mammals. Mammals are a type of animal which have furry or hairy skin and which feed their babies with their milk. They are also warm-blooded, which means that their bodies always stay at about the same temperature, even when the weather gets cold.

The dinosaurs became extinct about 65 million years ago. Then, free from the threat of the giant reptiles, the mammals came out from their hiding places in the daytime.

Some of the early mammals lived in trees, others were small rat-like creatures which scampered across the ground. There were strange flying squirrels and early kinds of rabbits too. Not all the animals living at this time were mammals though. Some reptiles, like snakes and lizards, survived the dinosaurs and are the ancestors of reptiles which are alive today.

Gradually, over millions of years, new kinds of mammals evolved. Many of them are now extinct, but palaeontologists have discovered their fossil remains. There were huge, plant-eating mammals, such as the giant *Brontotherium* ("thunder beast") and rhinoceroses nearly twice the size of a modern rhinoceros. There were grizzly cave bears, woolly mammoths with thick, shaggy coats and fierce, sabre-toothed cats.

By studying the fossils of prehistoric mammals, scientists have unravelled the history of many of the animals that are alive today. They have discovered how elephants evolved and how horses developed from small, four-toed creatures the size of dogs. They have even discovered how man, who is also a mammal, evolved from squirrel-like creatures which lived in the trees about 50 million years ago.

Life after the Dinosaurs

Animals which have fur or hair and give birth to babies are called mammals. The first mammals lived about 200 million years ago, at the same time as the dinosaurs. The dinosaurs were reptiles. Reptiles are animals which have scaly skin and lay eggs.

About 65 million years ago, all the dinosaurs died out. Then, gradually, different kinds of mammals developed. This picture shows some of the mammals which lived between 50 and 65 million years ago. They are the ancestors of mammals which are alive today.

Notharctus could climb trees and had sharp eyesight. It is an ancestor of modern lemurs and lived 50 million years ago.

The first horse lived about 50 million years ago. It is known as *Hyracotherium* and was only 40 cm high.

This creature is called *Planetetherium*. It could glide down from trees but could not fly properly.

Taeniolabus was about the size of a beaver. It had sharp, chisel-like teeth for gnawing tough plants.

Scientists have found only the skull of *Ctenacodon* and are not sure what its body looked like.

How we know

The remains of plants and animals which lived long ago have been preserved as fossils in the rocks.

Sometimes, when an animal died, its body was buried in mud or sand. The flesh soon rotted away but the bones and teeth remained.

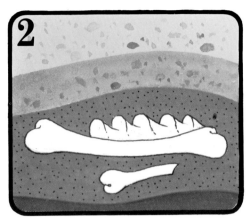

Over millions of years the mud and sand hardened to form rock. The bones and teeth changed too, and became fossils inside the rock.

Fossils are found when the rocks around them wear away. Scientists called palaeontologists study the fossils and find out about the animals which lived long ago.

What are mammals?

Animals which have backbones are divided into five groups. There are fish, amphibians, reptiles, birds and mammals. Scientists call these groups "classes".

All animals which have fur or hair, give birth to babies and feed them with their milk belong to the class of mammals.

Most animals have a common name and a scientific name in Latin or Greek. Animals' scientific names are written in *italics* in this book. There is a list of what these names mean in English on the last page.

Cows are mammals. The cow gives birth to a calf which feeds on its mother's milk and is protected by her until it is strong enough to look after itself.

Reptiles are very different from mammals. They have scaly skin and lay eggs. Snakes, crocodiles and lizards belong to the class of reptiles.

Reptiles do not usually look after their young. Crocodiles lay their eggs in a nest of plants by the river. When the eggs hatch the babies have to find their own food.

Mammals, such as the cat, can control the warmth of their bodies. Their body temperature stays about the same all the time. Mammals are called warm-blooded animals.

Reptiles cannot control the warmth of their bodies. Their temperature changes as the air around them gets hotter or colder. They are called cold-blooded animals.

Dolphins are mammals which live in the sea. They are warm-blooded and give birth to babies which they feed with their milk. Whales are mammals too.

Some mammals have very little hair. Elephants are mammals, though their hair is very thin, and man is also a mammal.

35

From Reptiles to Mammals

About 250 million years ago, most of the animals on the Earth were reptiles. A few of them, though, had some of the features of mammals.

Dimetrodon was about 3 m long. It had teeth like a mammal, but its scaly skin was like a reptile's. The sail on its back probably helped it to warm up in the sun.

Hiding from dinosaurs

The early mammals were probably nocturnal, they slept during the day and woke up at night. The cold-blooded dinosaurs became very sluggish and inactive in the cool night. While the dinosaurs slept, the tiny mammals could wander safely and eat insects and worms.

Cynognathus looked much more like a mammal. It was probably hairy, and its legs were tucked in under its body like a mammal's. It is called a mammal-like reptile.

Cynognathus was probably warm-blooded, but we do not know if it laid eggs or had babies. It was nearly 2 m long and lived about 220 million years ago.

Triconodon was one of the first mammals and lived about 190 million years ago. It was about the size of a cat and was probably furry and warm-blooded.

Scientists have found very few of its fossil bones. They do not know if it laid eggs or had babies, but it probably fed its young with its milk.

Fossil clues

There are very few fossils of animal's skin or eggs, but palaeontologists can tell whether an animal was a mammal or a reptile by looking at the fossil skulls.

Reptile's skull

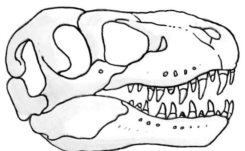

Reptiles have only one kind of teeth and their lower jaw is made of several bones.

Mammal's skull

Mammals have three different kinds of teeth and their lower jaw is made of one bone.

Tyrannosaurus rex

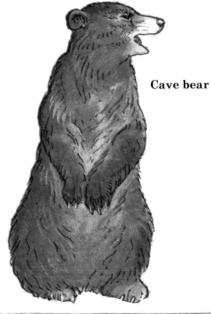

Cave bear

The meat-eating dinosaur *Tyrannosaurus rex* attacking *Triceratops*.

Purgatorius was a mammal. It was the size of a rat and lived about 70 million years ago. It was probably furry and may have laid eggs.

Mammal or reptile?

Here is the skull of an early plant-eating animal. Can you tell if it is a mammal or a reptile?

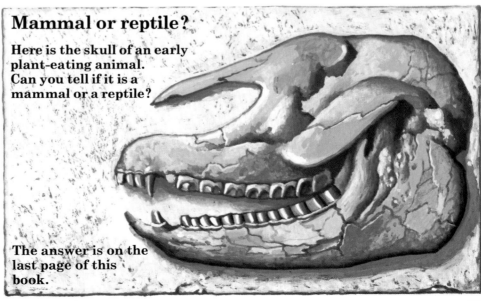

The answer is on the last page of this book.

Mammals with Pouches

The first mammals probably laid eggs like their ancestors, the reptiles. Later some mammals gave birth to very tiny babies. The babies crawled into a pouch on the mother's stomach and stayed there until they had grown. Mammals with pouches are called marsupial mammals.

Most mammals living now give birth to fully grown babies. They are called placental mammals. In Australia, though, there are still some marsupials and also some very primitive mammals which still lay eggs.

Primitive mammals alive today

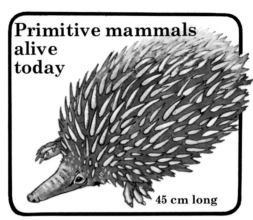

45 cm long

The spiny anteater, or *Echidna*, is a mammal which lays eggs. It has a long nose for digging in ant hills and stiff, prickly spines. It lives in Australia.

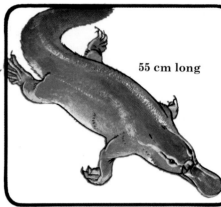

55 cm long

The duck-billed platypus has sleek hair and a horny bill. It lines its burrow with grass and lays two eggs. When the eggs hatch the babies drink their mother's milk.

1 What happened to marsupials?

Today, marsupial mammals are found only in Australia and America. The koala is a marsupial mammal. Its babies develop in the mother koala's pouch.

2

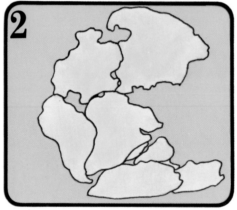

When the dinosaurs and the first mammals were alive, all the land was joined up. Then, about 150 million years ago, the continents began to slowly move apart.

3

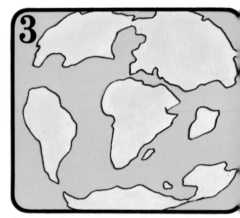

When Australia and America broke away from the rest of the land, there were no placental mammals anywhere. Marsupials lived on all the continents then.

4

Later, placental mammals developed in Europe and North America. They survived more easily than the marsupials, which eventually all died out.

5

Marsupial mammals survived in Australia because no placentals developed there. All the placentals now in Australia were taken there by people.

Marsupial and placental babies

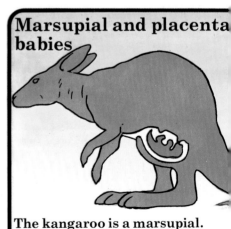

The kangaroo is a marsupial. When the baby kangaroo is born it is about the size of a bee. It crawls into the mother's pouch and is fed from her nipple.

Prehistoric mammals in Australia

All the prehistoric mammals in Australia were marsupials. There were no placental mammals until early people took dogs there and later settlers brought sheep and rabbits. Here are the ancestors of modern kangaroos and wombats.

Procoptoda was a giant kangaroo. It was about 3 m tall, nearly twice as tall as a modern kangaroo. Like modern kangaroos it was a marsupial mammal. It lived in Australia about a million years ago.

3 m long

Diprotodon was a marsupial mammal which lived at the same time as *Procoptoda*. It grazed on the plants which grew near salt lakes and is an ancestor of the modern wombat.

placenta

After eight months in the pouch the baby kangaroo has grown and looks like a little adult. It leaves the pouch, though it still feeds on its mother's milk for a while.

The rabbit is a placental mammal. Its babies develop in the uterus, inside the mother's body. Part of the mother's body, called the placenta, carries food to the baby.

When the baby rabbits are born the mother looks after them and feeds them with her milk. After about two weeks the babies are strong enough to leave the nest.

The Age of Mammals

When all the dinosaurs became extinct, there was more space on the land and mammals began to live in new places. Slowly, over several million years, they began to change. Some of them became suited to living in trees, and had hands which could grip the branches. Others adapted to life in the water and developed smooth, streamlined bodies. Some mammals began to eat only plants and others became meat-eaters. The way animals slowly change over millions of years is called evolution.

Earliest mammals

The earliest mammals which lived during the age of dinosaurs ate insects and were about the size of rats. All the later mammals evolved from animals like these.

about 60 cm long

Plesiadapis lived in trees about 55 million years ago and ate fruit and leaves. It is an ancestor of monkeys.

Where the mammals lived

Basilosaurus was a prehistoric whale. It was about 21 m long and lived 40 million years ago.

The ancestors of rats and mice lived 50 million years ago. These are called *Paramys*.

30 cm long

How animals evolve

In the animal world, only the fittest, strongest animals can survive. The weaker animals die.

Sometimes an animal is born slightly different from its parents. This difference may help it to survive and it may have babies like itself. These babies grow up and pass on their advantage to their offspring and eventually, all the animals in the group have it.

1 Lions eat meat and to survive they must be able to catch other animals for their food.

2 Zebras live together in herds to protect themselves from lions. It is the less alert animals which get caught.

3 The other zebras survive. They are alert or can run fast and pass these qualities to their offspring.

This is a bat called *Icaronycteris* which lived 50 million years ago. Bats are flying mammals. Many of them eat insects.

Fossil bat 12 cm long

Uintatherium was as large as a rhinoceros. It ate plants and had six bony lumps like horns on its skull.

3½ m long

Moeritherium was a prehistoric elephant. It was only the size of a pig and had no trunk.

2 m long

about 1 m long

These are prehistoric hares which lived about 38 million years ago. They are called *Palaeolagus*.

Mesonyx was a fierce little mammal which ate meat. It lived about 50 million years ago.

30 cm long

Spot the mammals

Here are some prehistoric mammals and reptiles. Can you tell which is which? The answers are on the last page of this book.

The sabre-toothed cat lived about a million years ago. It had long fangs for tearing meat.

This is *Triceratops*. It lived 100 million years ago and was about 11 m long.

Andrewsarchus lived 50 million years ago. It was about 4 m long.

Steneosaurus measured about 6 m from nose to tail. It lived 195 million years ago.

This is a prehistoric whale called *Basilosaurus*. It was over 20 m long and lived 40 million years ago.

41

Hunters and Scavengers

Most of the first mammals ate insects and worms. Later, as mammals evolved, some of them began to eat meat. Meat-eating animals are called carnivores.

Carnivores need to be quick and intelligent to catch their prey. They need claws to hold the animal and sharp teeth to tear the meat.

The early meat-eating mammals were not very clever or fast. They preyed on the herbivores, which were as slow and small-brained as themselves.

One of the early meat-eating mammals was *Oxyaena*. It lived about 50 million years ago. Here it is eating *Hyracotherium*, a prehistoric horse.

Cynodictis were prehistoric dogs. They lived about 30 million years ago and were less than 30 cm long, about the size of a weasel. They could not run very fast.

Monster bird

An enormous bird called *Diatryma* lived about 50 million years ago, at the same time as the early mammals.

Scavenging animal

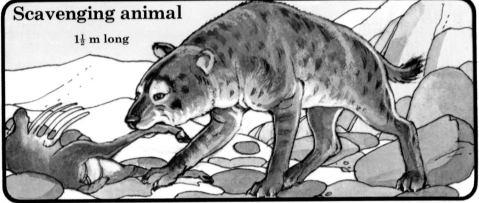

1½ m long

Hyaenas are scavengers. They eat the left-overs from the meals of other carnivores, and do not hunt for their own food. The first hyaenas lived 20 million years ago.

Hyaenas have very strong jaws and teeth so that they can crack open bones and eat the soft marrow inside. Sometimes they even eat rotten meat.

Teeth for tearing and crunching

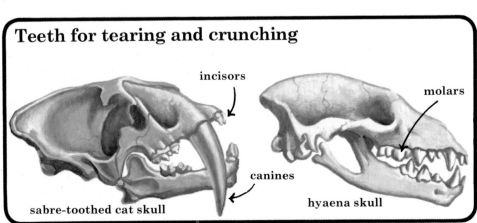

incisors

molars

canines

sabre-toothed cat skull

hyaena skull

These two fossil skulls show what carnivores' teeth were like. They had sharp incisor teeth for nipping, long dagger-like canines for tearing and molars for cutting.

The sabre-toothed cat was given its name because it had such long canines. The hyaena had large, strong molar teeth for crunching and breaking open bones.

They lived together in packs and the members of a pack hunted together and shared their prey. They could catch animals more easily together than by themselves.

Sabre-toothed cats first lived about 26 million years ago. They had long, stabbing teeth which they probably used to tear the thick skin of elephants.

There were many different kinds of sabre-toothed cats. This one is called *Machairodus*. Cats hunt by stalking their prey, pouncing on it and holding it with their claws.

2½ m long

Diatryma was about 3 m tall, which is nearly as tall as an African elephant. *Diatryma* ate meat and fed on small mammals. It could not fly and it became extinct about 45 million years ago.

Cave bear

The cave bear lived about 70,000 years ago, at the same time as stone-age people. It was larger than a modern brown bear and measured 3 m from nose to tail.

The cave bear ate meat and plants. It was a strong animal, but it could not run very fast to catch other animals. Animals which eat meat and plants are called omnivores.

3 m long

Mammals which Eat Plants

Animals which eat only plants are called herbivores. Plant-eating mammals evolved later than carnivorous mammals because plants are more difficult to digest than meat. The animals had to develop strong teeth with flat grinding surfaces to chew the plant food well.

Carnivores ate the herbivores, so they had to be able to protect themselves. Some of the herbivores developed horns or tusks. Others became fast runners with long legs, or lived together in herds for safety.

Barylambda was one of the first herbivorous mammals, living about 55 million years ago. It was a large animal about 3 m long, and it soon became extinct.

4 m long

Brontotherium was a huge beast about the size of a hippopotamus. It had a forked horn on the end of its nose to fend off the carnivores. Its name means "thunder-beast".

Giant mammal

This is a prehistoric rhinoceros called *Baluchitherium*. It is the tallest land mammal that has ever existed and it could reach leaves in the tree-tops. It lived about 25 million years ago.

8 m tall
11 m long

Prehistoric landscape

When the early mammals were alive, the Earth's climate was warmer than it is today. About 45 million years ago there were palm trees and crocodiles in Europe.

Magnolia flowers have thick, waxy petals. Nowadays they grow in warm, sheltered places.

Brontotherium ate leaves and soft fruit. Like other herbivores it had small canine teeth and large, grinding molar teeth. It lived about 8 million years ago.

Some modern herbivores have several parts in their stomachs. Each part helps to digest the tough plants. Prehistoric herbivores may have had stomachs like this too.

Alticamelus was a prehistoric camel about 3 m tall. Its long legs ended in hard hoofs which helped it to run away from carnivores like these wolves.

Many different kinds of birds evolved at the same time as the early mammals.

1¾ m long

Coryphodon ate leaves but it had sabre-like canines to defend itself.

Reptiles are cold-blooded, so most of them live in hot places where they can keep warm.

Some prehistoric tortoises were nearly a metre long.

Trapped ant

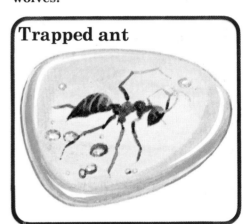

This ant was trapped in the sticky resin from a tree about 35 million years ago. The resin hardened to form amber and the ant became a fossil inside the amber.

Clues to plants

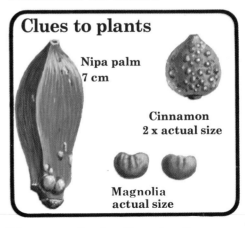

Nipa palm 7 cm

Cinnamon 2 x actual size

Magnolia actual size

These are the fossil seeds of some plants which grew about 50 million years ago. Seeds are the hardest part of a plant and they make good fossils.

45

Horns, Antlers and Claws

Many of the herbivorous mammals had horns, tusks or antlers to protect themselves from the carnivores. Some mammals, such as the deer, also used their antlers to fight amongst themselves and prove which of them was the strongest. Carnivores never evolved horns or antlers because they had their sharp teeth and claws to defend them.

Some herbivores had claws too, but they used them for digging and not for defending themselves.

1 Horns

Arsinoitherium had two large horns to defend itself. The horns were made of bone, covered with skin. They were quite light because the bone had lots of tiny spaces in it.

Arsinoitherium lived about 35 million years ago. It was a slow, heavy animal, about 3 m long and had strong legs and broad feet to support its weight.

1 Claws

Cats use their claws for holding and killing their prey. They can draw their claws back into sheaths of skin in their paws to keep them sharp. This is a sabre-toothed cat. It is sharpening its claws on a tree-trunk.

Antlers

Antlers are made of bone and they drop off every year. A new pair grows again very quickly.

2

Moropus was a plant-eating mammal which lived about 20 million years ago. It had strong, blunt claws which it used to dig up roots to eat. It was nearly 3 m tall and probably ate leaves from the trees too.

46

2½ m long

Arsinoitherium

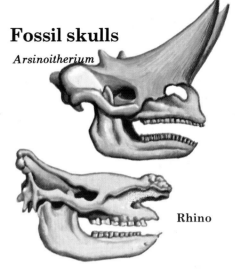

Rhino

These are prehistoric rhinoceroses called *Dicerorhinus*. They lived over [a] million years ago, and were not [a]s large as modern rhinos. The [b]aby has not yet grown its horns.

Rhinoceroses' horns are made of bundles of hair which become stuck together. The horns are very strong, but they do not make good fossils.

The lower fossil skull is from a prehistoric rhino which had only one horn. The horn did not become a fossil, but there is a lump on the skull where the horn grew.

Megaloceros was a giant deer which [h]ad antlers over 4 m wide. It lived [a]bout 20,000 years ago. Only the [m]ale animals had antlers and they [fo]ught together to win the females.

Make a prehistoric zoo

To make stand-up, paper models of prehistoric animals, you need paper, tracing paper, paints and scissors. On page 59 there are other animal patterns to trace.

Prehistoric footprint

This is the fossil of the footprint [o]f a prehistoric deer. It had two [t]oes with hard hoofs which helped [it] to run fast. The two toes show [c]learly on the fossil.

SLIT HEAD AND PUT ANTLERS IN SLIT

Fold a piece of paper in half. Trace the deer and antlers on to the paper with its back on the fold. Paint them and then cut them out with the paper still folded.

Make a small slit in the top of the deer's head and then open the paper so that the deer stands up.

Pattern for sabre-toothed cat

The Story of the Elephant

The first elephants lived about 40 million years ago. They did not look much like elephants. They had no trunks or tusks and were only the size of pigs.

Over millions of years, as elephants evolved, they became larger and heavier. This helped to protect them from small carnivores. They also developed long trunks.

There were lots of different prehistoric elephants, but most of them became extinct. Now, there are only two kinds of elephant, the African elephant and the Indian elephant.

1 m tall

Moeritherium is the earliest elephant known. It lived in swamps about 40 million years ago and ate soft, juicy plants. It was about the size of a large pig.

It hid in the water when it was in danger. Its eyes and ears were high on its head so it could see and hear even when the rest of its body was under the water.

1 Elephants' trunks

The earliest elephants had long noses but no real trunks or tusks. They were only about a metre tall and ate plants.

Later elephants were larger. They did not evolve long necks to reach their food as some other animals did, because their heads were too heavy.

Instead the elephant's upper lip and nose became very long and made a trunk which elephants use for feeding and drinking.

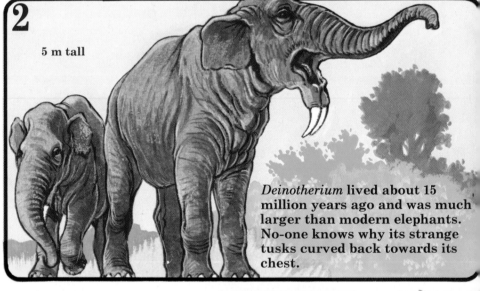

5 m tall

Deinotherium lived about 15 million years ago and was much larger than modern elephants. No-one knows why its strange tusks curved back towards its chest.

about 1½ m tall

Gomphotherium had short tusks on its upper and lower jaws. It lived about 6 million years ago and had special teeth with sharp points for grinding the leaves it ate.

Digging up clues

This is the fossil of an elephant which lived about six million years ago.

4

about 2 m tall

Platybelodon lived about 5 million years ago. It had two short, sharp tusks in its upper jaw and shovel-like tusks in its lower jaw. It used these for pulling up plants from soft, muddy ground.

5

5 m tall

Palaeoloxodon lived in forests in Europe, Asia and Africa about 250,000 years ago. It was a huge elephant, up to 5 m tall. Like modern elephants it probably had very little hair.

49

How Horses Evolved

When the first horses lived, about 50 million years ago, the land was covered with thick forests. Then, very gradually, the climate became cooler. The forests disappeared and grass grew instead.

The horses had to change so that they could survive in the grasslands. Over millions of years they became larger and able to run fast to get away from carnivores in the open countryside. Their teeth also evolved, so that they could eat tough grass instead of soft leaves.

40 cm tall

The earliest horses lived about 50 million years ago and are called *Hyracotherium*. They were about the size of foxes and had large nails instead of hoofs.

Hyracotherium lived in the forests. They had four toes on their front feet and three on their back feet. Their toes were spread out and helped them walk on soft ground.

Prehistoric ancestors

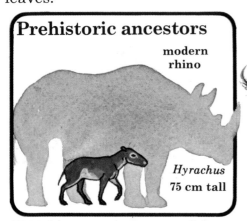

modern rhino

Hyrachus
75 cm tall

Hyrachus was an ancestor of the rhino. It was about the size of a pig, could run fast and had no horns. It lived about 40 million years ago.

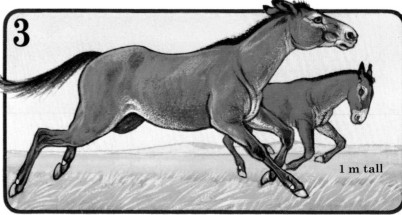

1 m tall

By about 10 million years ago the horses were nearly 1 m tall. They are called *Merychippus*. They ate grass and could run fast across the plains to escape from danger.

Merychippus had developed hard hoofs on their middle toes which helped them to run fast. Their other toes were much shorter and they walked on the middle toes.

Different kinds of horses

modern camel

Stenomylus
75 cm tall

Stenomylus was a small prehistoric camel. It lived about 20 million years ago and was about as big as a goat. We do not know whether it had a hump or not.

Mountain pony

People first domesticated horses about 4,000 years ago. Since then man has bred many different kinds of horses. Short, stocky mountain ponies can live in cold places.

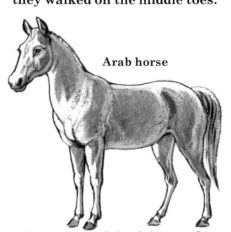

Arab horse

Long-legged Arab horses have been bred as racing horses. Carthorses are strong, powerful animals which can pull heavy loads.

2

75 cm tall

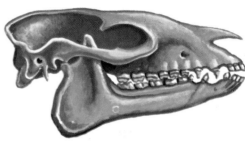

Horse skulls

Hyracotherium had small, knobbly teeth. It ate soft tree leaves and did not need large teeth to chew them.

he horses which lived about 35 illion years ago were larger than *Hyracotherium*. They are called *Mesohippus* and had three toes on ll their feet.

Mesohippus lived when the forests were disappearing and there was more grassland. Its middle toes were larger than the others to bear its weight on hard ground.

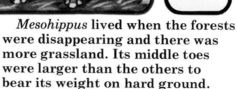

4

1¼ m tall

Equus has sharp, nipping teeth at the front for cutting through grass stems, and large ridged molars for crushing the grass before it swallows it.

Modern horses first lived about 3 illion years ago. Their scientific ame is *Equus*. Each foot has only ne toe which ends with a large, ard hoof.

Equus can run very fast on their hard hoofs. Their side toes have become tiny bones under the skin near the top of their feet. Very few wild horses still live today.

How hoofs evolved

If you put your hand flat on the ground, your four fingers touch the ground, as *Hyracotherium's* toes did. Now lift the palm of your hand off the ground and your little finger no longer touches. If you go on lifting your palm, only the middle finger will be left touching the ground.

This is what happened as horses grew larger. They began to run on the tips of their toes, then on only their middle toes which became covered with tough hoofs to make them stronger.

Carthorse

To breed a horse you have to hoose two parent horses with ome of the qualities you want. heir foal will have some qualities rom both parents.

Why horses need shoes

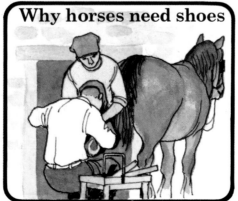

Horses' hoofs are made of a thick material like fingernails. This slowly wears away on modern road surfaces, so their hoofs have to be covered with metal shoes.

Darwin's Trip to South America

In 1831, a ship called the *Beagle* was sent to map the coast of South America. On board there was a young scientist called Charles Darwin.

When the ship anchored, Darwin went ashore to explore the countryside. On the beach he found fossil bones of strange animals.

Along the shore at the foot of the cliffs, Darwin found fossil skulls, claws and a tusk. They were the fossils of extinct animals and Darwin was very curious.

All night long Darwin and a friend dug up fossils. By dawn they had piles of fossil bones stacked on the beach and they took them back to the ship to study.

Why South America was different

During the age of mammals, North and South America were not joined. Many kinds of mammals evolved in South America which did not exist in the North.

North America

South America

About 5 million years ago volcanoes erupted and made the bit of land that joins North and South America.

When North and South America were joined, mammals from North America moved south. They were more able to survive than the South American mammals which slowly died out.

Strange mammals in South America

These are some of the strange animals which lived in South America until about 20,000 years ago.

2½ m long

Thylacosmilus was a marsupial mammal. It ate meat and had huge canine teeth like the sabre-toothed cat, although it was no relation.

3½ m long

Macrauchenia was as large as a camel. It may have used its short trunk to eat or smell with. Each of its toes had a little hoof and it was a fast runner.

3

Darwin had discovered the fossils of prehistoric animals that had become extinct. Later, he wrote a book on the evolution of animals called "The Origin of Species".

Giant sloth

Megatherium was a giant ground sloth which lived in South America 15,000 years ago.

6 m long

Megatherium had long, twisted claws and could not put its feet flat on the ground. It walked on the side of its feet and reared up on its haunches to eat leaves.
It was as large as an elephant.

Phororhacos was a meat-eating bird over 2 m tall.
It could not fly because its wings were too small, but it could run quite fast.

Daedicurus had thick bony plates and spikes on its tail to protect it from carnivores. It could not move very fast and ate insects, worms and berries.

2¾ m long

Make an armoured *Daedicurus*

1 BODY → PRESS ON HEAD, TAIL AND LEGS **2**

THIN PIECE OF PLASTICINE

You will need plasticine, some dried peas or lentils and a bit of card. First make a plasticine body, as in the picture above.

Roll out a thin, flat piece of plasticine to fit over the body. Then trim the edges with scissors to make it the right shape.

3 PLASTICINE EARS   LENTILS OR PEAS **4**

MAKE MARKINGS WITH A PENCIL

Put a small, flat piece of plasticine on its head, and two little ears. Then press the dried peas or lentils into the plasticine.

Cut five small spikes of card and stick them in the tail. Then mark the mouth with a pencil and use lentils or peas for eyes.

The Ice Ages

Several times during the last million years, northern parts of the world have been buried under thick ice. For thousands of years the winters were very long and cold and the snow and ice never melted. These long ice ages are called glacials and the warmer periods in between are called interglacials.

During the glacials, animals which could not survive the cold moved south to warmer places. Other animals, such as the mammoth, slowly evolved and changed so that they could live in the cold.

A solid mass of ice which moves slowly down a mountain is called a glacier. Glaciers covered much of the land in the ice ages, and they still exist in high mountains.

The land near the edge of the ice was very cold. Only mosses, lichens and small bushes grew there. Cold places where few plant will grow are called tundra.

2 m tall

Herds of reindeer and bison lived near the ice and grazed on the tundra plants. They had thick fur and were able to survive the icy cold.

In summer the snow melted and the ground was very muddy. The reindeer had hoofs on their toes and wide feet which helped them to walk on the mud and snow.

Surviving the cold

Woolly mammoths were a kind of elephant which adapted to live in the ice age. They had long, woolly hair and a thick layer of fat under their skin to keep them warm.

Between the ice ages

5 m tall

During the interglacials the weather was warmer and rhinos and hippos lived in northern Europe. The animals which liked the cold moved further north.

Forests of oak trees grew and there were straight-tusked elephants. During the interglacials the climate in Europe was warmer than it is today.

Animals such as the arctic hare lived in the tundra and ate the mosses and lichens. There were wolves too, which ate the hares and other herbivores.

about 4½ m tall

Their tusks were long and curved and they probably used them to clear away snow and uncover plants to eat. Cave men hunted the woolly mammoths for their meat.

Make a woolly mammoth

You will need some newspaper, torn into small pieces, an old stocking, 12 pipecleaners, two buttons, a needle and thread.

1

TORN-UP NEWSPAPER

Cut the stocking so that it is about 20 cm long. Then stuff it with newspaper. Put very little in the toe and stuff the rest firmly.

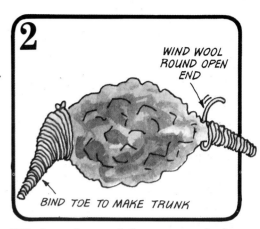

2 WIND WOOL ROUND OPEN END

BIND TOE TO MAKE TRUNK

Wind wool round the open end of the stocking to make the tail. Then bind the toe end to make the trunk and head, as shown in the picture.

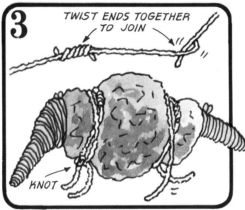

3 TWIST ENDS TOGETHER TO JOIN

KNOT

Join three pipecleaners and wrap them round the body behind the head. Tie in a knot underneath and leave the ends to make the legs. Repeat for the back legs.

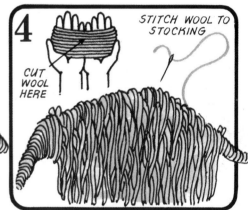

4 STITCH WOOL TO STOCKING

CUT WOOL HERE

Wind wool round a friend's hands and then cut one side of the wool to make lots of pieces. Put the wool over the mammoth's back and stitch on to the stocking.

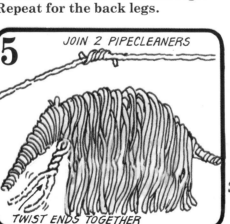

5 JOIN 2 PIPECLEANERS

TWIST ENDS TOGETHER

Join two pipecleaners and poke through the wool near the trunk. Make the ends the same length and twist them round each other. Do this again for the other tusk.

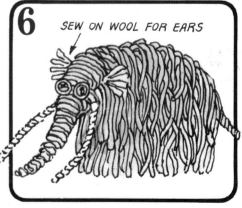

6 SEW ON WOOL FOR EARS

Sew on the buttons for eyes and a few short pieces of wool for the mammoth's ears. Then make sure the legs are the same length so the mammoth will stand up.

Fossils from the Ice Age

Palaeontologists know a lot about animals that lived during the ice ages. They have found the bodies of mammoths perfectly preserved in the ice, and woolly rhinos preserved in a mixture of oil and salt. These remains are also called fossils.

The frozen fossils show that mammoths had dark brown hair and their ears were small so that they did not lose heat from them. Some mammoths even had their last meal of tundra plants preserved in their stomachs.

1 Frozen mammoths

Herds of mammoths grazed on the tundra plants that grew during the short summer months. They wandered across the ice looking for more food.

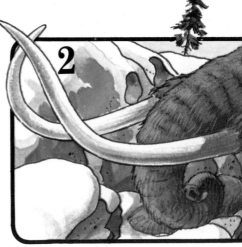

2

Sometimes, water from the melting snow washed away the soil under the ice. When mammoths walked on the ice it caved in and they were too heavy to pull themselves out.

Clues in caves

During the long ice-age winters some animals hibernated in caves. They slept through the cold months when there was very little to eat. Palaeontologists have found lots of clues to ice-age animals in caves.

Preserved rhino

about 2½ m long

This body of a woolly rhino was dug out of the ground in the U.S.S.R. It was buried in mud mixed with oil and salt and these prevented the body from rotting.

It is the body of a female rhino which died when it sank in deep mud. The flesh, skin and soft parts of the body were well preserved, but the horns were missing.

Cave hyaenas dragged the carcases of dead animals into caves to eat. The bones they left became fossils.

These are the fossil wings of caddis flies. They became fossils in the rock of a stalagmite on the floor of the cave.

Woolly rhinos

Woolly rhinos became extinct about 20,000 years ago. They ate the tundra plants and had two large horns to defend themselves from wolves and other carnivores.

They had thick hair and were well protected against the cold. Their feet were splayed out so that they could walk more easily on the soft, snowy ground.

When the weather got colder, the mammoths were frozen into the ice. Their bodies did not rot away, though they were sometimes attacked by wolves.

Mammoths' bodies have lasted for thousands of years in the ice. About 25 frozen mammoths have been found in Siberia, in the U.S.S.R., where it is still very cold.

Some of the mammoth meat was fed to the dogs which pulled the sleighs. But it began to rot soon after it was dug out of the frozen ground.

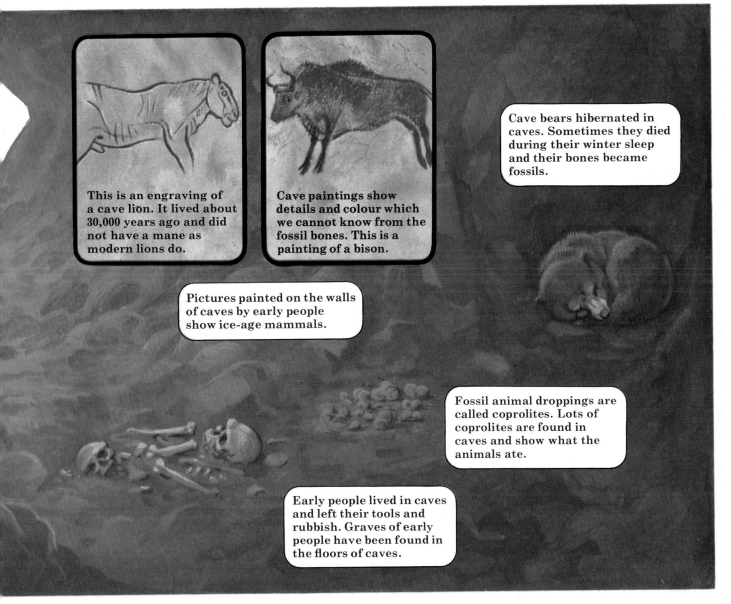

This is an engraving of a cave lion. It lived about 30,000 years ago and did not have a mane as modern lions do.

Cave paintings show details and colour which we cannot know from the fossil bones. This is a painting of a bison.

Cave bears hibernated in caves. Sometimes they died during their winter sleep and their bones became fossils.

Pictures painted on the walls of caves by early people show ice-age mammals.

Fossil animal droppings are called coprolites. Lots of coprolites are found in caves and show what the animals ate.

Early people lived in caves and left their tools and rubbish. Graves of early people have been found in the floors of caves.

Drowned in Tar

Thousands of fossil bones have been dug up at Rancho La Brea in Los Angeles, U.S.A. There are fossils of sabre-toothed cats, vultures, ground sloths and elephants.

These animals died in sticky pools of tar about 15,000 years ago. The tar seeped up from below the ground and was covered with a layer of rain-water. Animals went to the pools to drink and some of them leaned too far and fell into the tar. The tar hardened slowly and their bones were preserved as fossils.

1

About 15,000 years ago there were grassy plains where the city of Los Angeles now stands. Bison, elephants, ground sloths and sabre-toothed cats lived there.

The animals went down to the pools to drink. Carnivores lay waiting by the pools, ready to pounce and eat any animal that fell into the tar.

2 Animals struggling in the tar made an easy meal for the carnivores. But sometimes carnivores, such as the sabre-toothed cat, were too eager and fell into the tar themselves. It was mostly the younger animals which became trapped in the tar, as older animals had learned the dangers.

Smilodon was a sabre-toothed cat larger than a tiger. Over a thousand *Smilodon* fossils were found in the tar.

3 m long

Teratornis was a huge vulture which swooped down to eat the rotting flesh of dead animals.

3 m wing-span

Dire wolves went to the tar pools for an easy meal. They had strong jaws and teeth and could crunch up bones.

The Imperial mammoth was a species of elephant. It floundered in the tar until it was exhausted and the carnivores attacked it.

Fossil vulture

This fossil skeleton of the vulture *Teratornis* was found at Rancho La Brea. *Teratornis* had a strong, hooked beak with which it tore the meat it ate.

1 How oil is made

Tar comes from oil and oil is made when tiny plants and animals rot in the sand at the bottom of the sea.

2

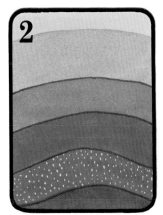

The sand slowly hardens to become rock. The little drops of oil are trapped in tiny spaces in the rock.

3

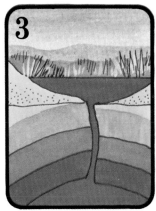

Sometimes oil seeps through cracks in the rock and oozes up to the surface. This happened at Rancho La Brea.

Rancho La Brea today

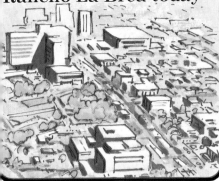

Rancho La Brea is now surrounded by the city of Los Angeles. People can go to visit the tar pits in Hancock Park and see models of the prehistoric mammals.

Fossil of the future

Animals in the park still fall in the tar and drown. This gopher is struggling in the sticky tar and may become a fossil in thousands of years time.

More prehistoric zoo animals

Here are some more patterns to trace to make stand-up paper animals. You can find out how to make them on page 47. You could copy other prehistoric animals from the book and make models of them them too.

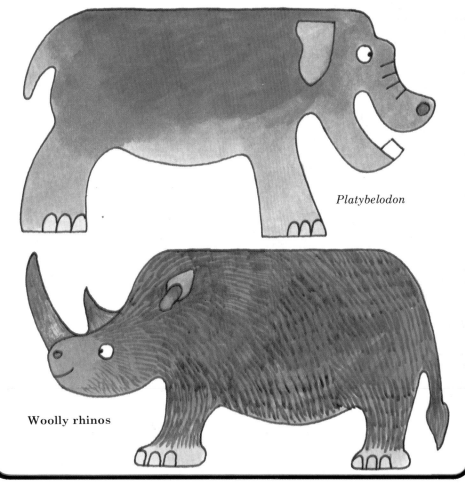

Platybelodon

Woolly rhinos

59

Why Animals Die Out

The strange mammals which lived in prehistoric times have become extinct. We know about them only because we have found their fossil remains.

These animals had evolved and become well suited to their surroundings. But then, very slowly, the climate and plants changed. The animals were not suited to survive in the new landscape. Many of them died and their numbers grew less and less until eventually the whole species, or group of animals became extinct.

Oxyaena hunted slow, plant-eating mammals. As the herbivores became gradually larger and faster, *Oxyaena* died out because it could not catch its prey.

The giant *Baluchitherium* ate leave from the tree-tops.When the forests disappeared *Baluchitherium* was too large and slow to survive in the grasslands.

Animals in danger

Many modern animals are threatened with extinction because of man's activities.

Poisonous chemicals, the spread of towns and hunting sports are killing our wildlife.

Saving wildlife

To help save animals, scientist have to study them. They find out how the animals live and how they will be affected by changes in their surroundings.

Leopards and the other wild cats have long been hunted for their beautiful furs. There are now very few wild cats, but laws have been passed to protect them.

Many of the animals that are killed are not needed for man's survival. Elephants are hunted for their ivory tusks and whale meat is used to make pet food.

This polar bear was shot with drugged darts so that the scientists could catch and study it.

The survival of gorillas and other animals is threatened as the forests where they live are cut down. The land is used to build towns and roads.

Land is also cleared to make farmland to feed the growing number of people on Earth. The animals cannot survive when their home has been destroyed.

milodon and the other sabre-toothed cats evolved to hunt the large elephants. When most of the elephants became extinct, the sabre-toothed cats died out too.

Woolly mammoths adapted to live in the cold ice age. When the climate became warmer at the end of the ice age, woolly mammoths became extinct.

People have helped to make many animals extinct. Early man hunted and killed mammoths and woolly rhinos for their meat and skins.

Nature reserves

To protect wild animals, large areas of land are made into nature reserves. There is no hunting or building in the reserve and the animals live there safely.

In no danger

There have been rats and mice on Earth for about 50 million years and they are in no danger of becoming extinct. They live on the rubbish made by people.

Zoos

Many wild animals are kept in zoos where people can go to see them. But this does not help save them from extinction, as wild animals are hard to breed in zoos.

Did you know?

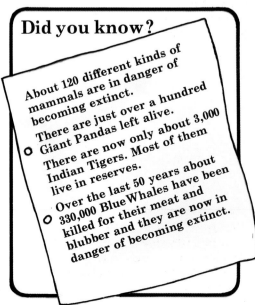

About 120 different kinds of mammals are in danger of becoming extinct.

There are just over a hundred Giant Pandas left alive.

○ There are now only about 3,000 Indian Tigers. Most of them live in reserves.

○ Over the last 50 years about 330,000 Blue Whales have been killed for their meat and blubber and they are now in danger of becoming extinct.

Time Chart:
The age of mammals

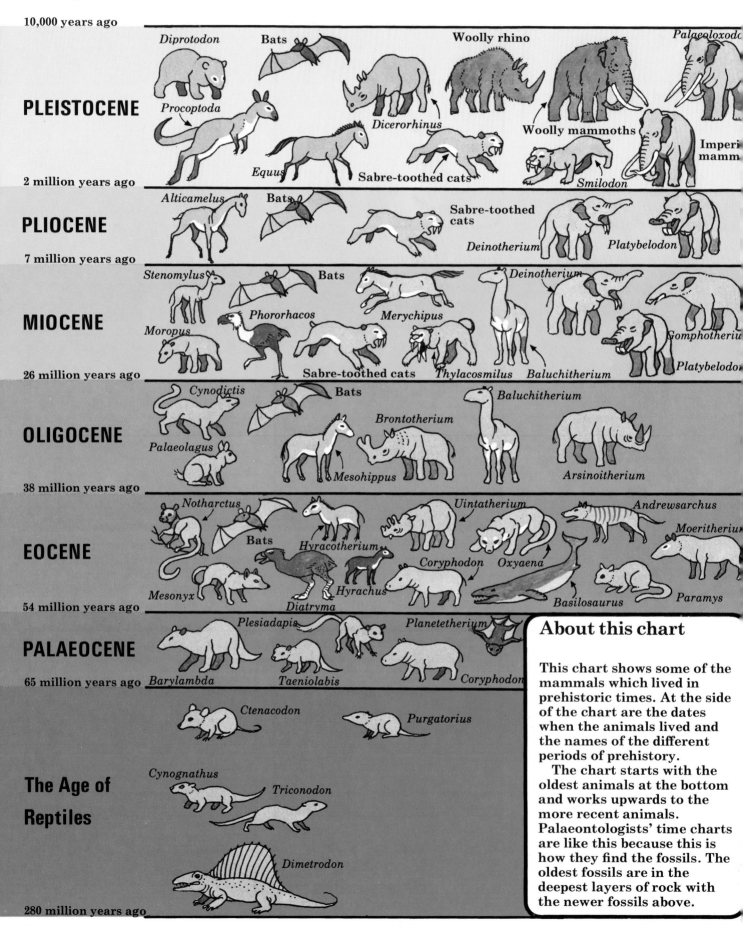

10,000 years ago

PLEISTOCENE

Diprotodon — Bats — Woolly rhino — *Palaeoloxodo*
Procoptoda
Dicerorhinus
Equus — Sabre-toothed cats — Woolly mammoths — *Smilodon* — Imperi mamm

2 million years ago

PLIOCENE

Alticamelus — Bats — Sabre-toothed cats — *Deinotherium* — *Platybelodon*

7 million years ago

MIOCENE

Stenomylus — Bats — *Deinotherium* — *Phororhacos* — *Merychipus* — *Moropus* — *Gomphotheriu* — *Platybelodo* — Sabre-toothed cats — *Thylacosmilus* — *Baluchitherium*

26 million years ago

OLIGOCENE

Cynodictis — Bats — *Baluchitherium* — *Brontotherium* — *Palaeolagus* — *Mesohippus* — *Arsinoitherium*

38 million years ago

EOCENE

Notharctus — *Uintatherium* — *Andrewsarchus* — Bats — *Hyracotherium* — *Moeritheriu* — *Coryphodon* — *Oxyaena* — *Mesonyx* — *Hyrachus* — *Diatryma* — *Basilosaurus* — *Paramys*

54 million years ago

PALAEOCENE

Plesiadapis — *Planetetherium* — *Barylambda* — *Taeniolabis* — *Coryphodon*

65 million years ago

Ctenacodon — *Purgatorius*

The Age of Reptiles

Cynognathus — *Triconodon* — *Dimetrodon*

280 million years ago

About this chart

This chart shows some of the mammals which lived in prehistoric times. At the side of the chart are the dates when the animals lived and the names of the different periods of prehistory.

The chart starts with the oldest animals at the bottom and works upwards to the more recent animals. Palaeontologists' time charts are like this because this is how they find the fossils. The oldest fossils are in the deepest layers of rock with the newer fossils above.

62

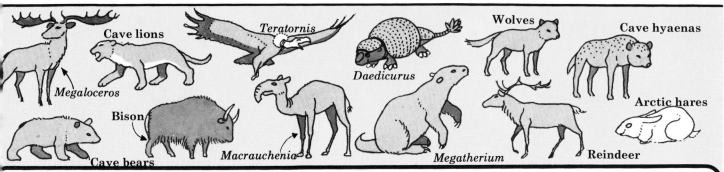

Megaloceros · Cave lions · Teratornis · Daedicurus · Wolves · Cave hyaenas · Bison · Macrauchenia · Megatherium · Reindeer · Arctic hares · Cave bears

Largest and Longest

Baluchitherium

The largest land mammal that has ever existed was *Baluchitherium*. It lived 25 million years ago and was 8.23 m tall and 11 m long. The tallest living mammal is the giraffe, which is 6 m tall.

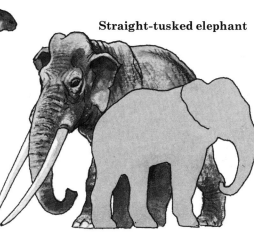

Straight-tusked elephant

The prehistoric straight-tusked elephant is the largest elephant that has ever lived. It was nearly 5 m tall. The largest modern elephant is the African elephant which is about 4 m tall.

The longest fossil tusk ever found belonged to a straight-tusked elephant. It was 5 m long. The longest tusks of an African elephant are 3.49 m long.

Elephant bird

Rugby ball

The prehistoric elephant bird was about 3.04 m tall. Its eggs were 86 cm long, which is three times longer than a rugby ball. The largest modern bird is the North African Ostrich, 2.74 m tall.

Basilosaurus

The longest of all prehistoric mammals was *Basilosaurus*. It was 21.33 m long. The modern blue whale is even longer. It is about 33.58 m long.

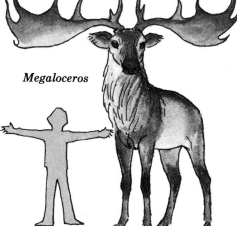

Megaloceros

Megaloceros, a prehistoric deer, had the widest horns of any animal yet discovered. They were 4.3 m wide.

63

The Story of Man

Like all the other animals on Earth today, man has evolved from prehistoric animals which lived millions of years ago. The earliest ancestors of man were small, furry creatures which lived 200 million years ago, at the same time as the dinosaurs.

Very, very gradually, these creatures evolved and changed. About 30 million years ago, when strange beasts like *Brontotherium* and the giant mammal *Baluchitherium* were alive, man's ancestors were monkey-like animals living in the forests.

Palaeontologists have found only a few fossils of man's early ancestors and do not yet know the whole story of how man evolved. But, as millions of years went by, the monkey-like creatures left the trees and began to live on the ground.

By about five million years ago, man's ancestors were probably hairy, ape-like creatures, about 1.25 m tall. They lived on grassy plains and had to defend themselves from fierce meat-eating animals. They caught small animals to eat and collected berries and leaves too.

Gradually they discovered how to use and make tools by chipping away pieces of stone. This helped them to kill animals much larger and stronger than themselves.

Palaeontologists have uncovered camps where man's ancestors lived over a million years ago. They have found their tools, bones of the animals they ate and rubbish they dropped. Gradually, as palaeontologists put together the fossil evidence they are finding out how man's ancestors left the animal world and became the first people.

Man's Ancestors

The first people lived about three million years ago, but they did not learn to farm or make tools of metal until less than 11,000 years ago. For hundreds of thousands of years, these people lived in caves and hunted for their food. They made tools from stones and antlers and wore animal skins to keep them warm.

These pictures take you back through the story of man to our earliest ancestors. These lived about 150 million years ago, at the same time as the dinosaurs.

Today, most of our food is grown by farmers with machines to help them sow and harvest the crops. Early people hunted for their food. They did not know how to farm.

People learned how to plant seeds and grow crops about 11,000 years ago. They collected the crop by hand and cut it with sickles which had flint blades.

About 350,000 years ago, people first learned how to make fire and use it to cook and keep warm. The earliest people were probably afraid of fire.

The first people lived about three million years ago. They learned how to make rough tools from stones by chipping them to give sharp edges.

About 14 million years ago there were no people on Earth. Monkey-like creatures, which were ancestors of man, lived in the tree and ate fruit.

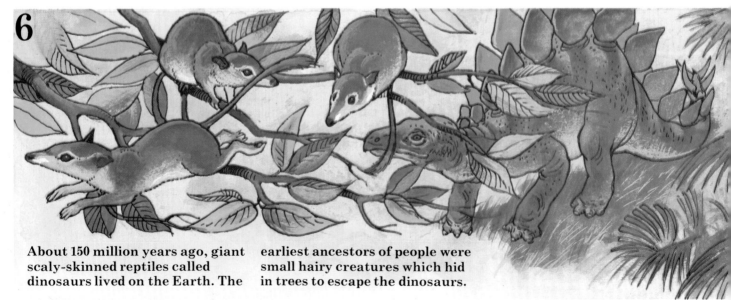

About 150 million years ago, giant scaly-skinned reptiles called dinosaurs lived on the Earth. The earliest ancestors of people were small hairy creatures which hid in trees to escape the dinosaurs.

Man's Relatives

People are mammals and they belong to a group of mammals called the primates. Monkeys, gorillas and chimpanzees are also primates. All the primates, including man, evolved from small, prehistoric primates which ate insects and lived in trees about 65 million years ago. Here are some modern primates.

40 cm long

Modern tree shrews look like the first prehistoric primates. They eat insects and live in trees in Asia.

120 cm long

Lemurs are found only on the island of Madagascar. This is a ring-tailed lemur.

about 1 m long

Baboons are another kind of monkey. They live together in troops and are found in Africa.

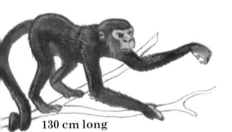

130 cm long

Spider monkeys live in the tallest trees in the forest and can grip with their tails. They live in South America.

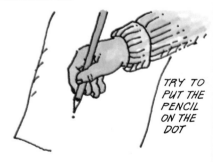

120–150 cm tall

Chimpanzees belong to the family of apes. They are more closely related to man than the other primates. They live in Africa.

Primates' special features

The primates developed so that they could survive in the trees. They have hands which can grip branches and good eyesight for judging distances.

People inherited these features from their monkey-like ancestors. Man has good eyesight and hands which can grip tools.

Bushbaby

The long fingers and toes of primates can curl round and grip branches. No other animals have hands and feet like those of the primates.

Gorilla

Primates see a separate picture with each of their eyes. Their brains put the two pictures together. This is called stereoscopic vision.

Test for stereoscopic vision

You can try this test for stereoscopic vision to see how it helps you to judge distances.

TRY TO PUT THE PENCIL ON THE DOT

Mark a dot on a piece of paper and stand about 60 cm away from it. Close one eye and try to put the point of a pencil on the dot without hesitating. Try with the other eye and then see how much easier it is with both your eyes open.

Early Primates

Scientists have found very few fossils of prehistoric primates, but they think that one, which they call *Ramapithecus*, was an ancestor of man. Another prehistoric primate, called *Dryopithecus*, was probably the ancestor of modern apes.

When these primates were alive about 12 million years ago, the climate was becoming cooler. Forests were getting smaller and grass grew instead. It was probably at this time that man's ancestors started living on the ground instead of in trees.

Man's ancestor

Fossil teeth

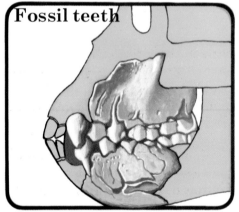

This is part of the fossil jaw of *Ramapithecus*. The jaw and teeth are shaped more like a human's than an ape's and scientists think it was an ancestor of man.

Ramapithecus lived in the trees in forests between six and 14 million years ago. They were about the size of monkeys and were probably good climbers.

At some stage, man's ancestors began to live on the ground and walk on two legs. *Ramapithecus* may sometimes have climbed down from the trees and run across the ground.

1 How fossils were made

When an animal died, it was sometimes covered with layers of mud and sand or with lava from a volcano. Its flesh rotted away, leaving its skull, bones and teeth.

2

Very, very slowly the mud and sand or lava hardened to form rock. The skull, bones and teeth were preserved in the rock. They are the fossils that are found today.

When they lived

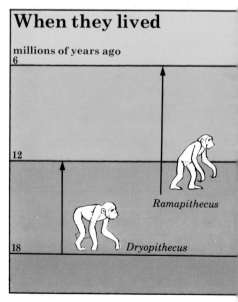

millions of years ago
6

12

18

Ramapithecus

Dryopithecus

68

Prehistoric ape

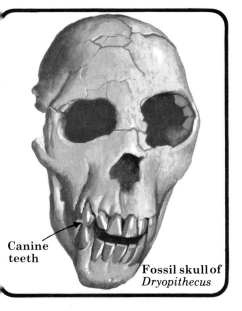

Canine teeth

Fossil skull of *Dryopithecus*

This is a prehistoric primate called *Dryopithecus*. Scientists think it may have been the ancestor of modern apes because it had long, ape-like canine teeth.

Dryopithecus lived in forests around 14 million years ago. The skull of *Dryopithecus* shown on the right was slightly crushed as it became fossilized.

Clues from teeth

The shape of the fossil jaws of *Ramapithecus* show that it was related to man. The sides of the jaws slope outwards, like man's. The jaws of *Dryopithecus* are more like those of a modern ape and have straight sides.

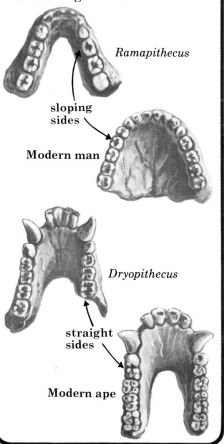

Ramapithecus

sloping sides

Modern man

Dryopithecus

straight sides

Modern ape

How primates evolved

The prehistoric primates evolved in the trees and developed special gripping hands and good eyesight to help them survive.

Gradually, as the primates evolved, they adapted to life in different parts of the trees. Now small, light monkeys live in the tops of the trees. The heavier apes live in the lower branches and the large baboons and gorillas live most of the time on the ground.

Living in different parts of the trees helps them to survive because they are not all competing for the same food.

Chimpanzees live on the ground and in the trees and are good climbers.

Colobus monkeys can climb and jump safely in the highest branches.

Baboons live on the ground. The fierce males defend the troop from attack by leopards.

The Near-Men

About three million years ago creatures we call hominids were living on the grassy plains in Africa. The name hominid comes from the Latin word *homo*, which means man.

There were two different kinds of hominids living at that time. One of them was a direct ancestor of man and is called *Homo*. The other is called *Australopithecus*. There were several different kinds of *Australopithecus*. The hominids probably could not talk and had not yet become people.

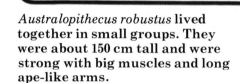

Australopithecus robustus lived together in small groups. They were about 150 cm tall and were strong with big muscles and long ape-like arms.

They had large teeth and strong jaws for chewing tough plants. The brain of *Australopithecus* was about half the size of modern man's brain.

Fossil skulls of hominids

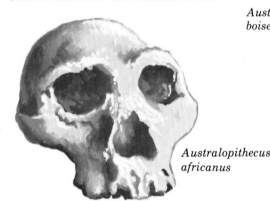

Australopithecus africanus

Like the other early hominids, *Australopithecus africanus* had a thick ridge of bone above his eyes. His brain case was small.

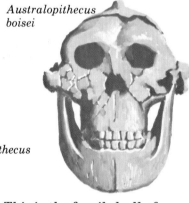

Australopithecus boisei

This is the fossil skull of *Australopithecus boisei*, another kind of *Australopithecus*. He had very large jaws and a ridge of bone on top of his head.

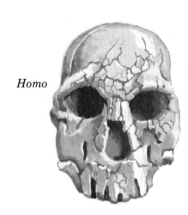

Homo

Homo had a larger brain than *Australopithecus* and so his skull was rounder on top. When the skull was put together, missing pieces were filled in with blue plaster.

Life on the plains

Australopithecus and *Homo* probably lived together in the same place. They could live in the same area because they ate different kinds of food.

When they lived

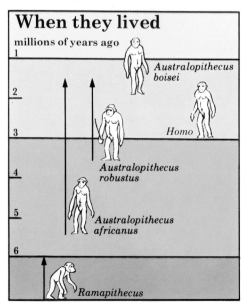

millions of years ago

1

Australopithecus boisei

2

Homo

3

Australopithecus robustus

4

Australopithecus africanus

5

6

Ramapithecus

2

AFRICA

Hadar •

Lake Turkana • Koobi
Fora

Lake Victoria
• Olduvai
Gorge

**All the fossils
of these
hominids were
found in South
and East Africa.**

• Sterkfontein
Swartkrans

ustralopithecus africanus were only
bout 120 cm tall. They had smaller
eeth than *robustus* and ate meat
hich is easier to digest and needs
ess chewing than plants.

They caught small animals to eat.
They probably used branches or
stones to kill their prey and to
defend themselves from other
animals on the plains.

Small groups of *Homo* probably hunted
animals to eat. Stone tools over $2\frac{1}{2}$
millions years old have been found, but
palaeontologists do not know which
hominid made them.

Australopithecus robustus ate
erries, leaves and fruits. They
id not know how to store food and
ad to move around to find enough
o eat every day.

They may have pushed twigs into
a termites' nest to pull out the
small white grubs and eat them.
Modern chimpanzees eat termites
like this.

Australopithecus robustus
probably dug up roots with sticks
and took birds eggs and ate them
raw. Palaeontologists do not know
if they made tools or not.

71

The First People

About 1¾ million years ago, small groups of people lived by the side of a lake in East Africa. These people were our direct ancestors. They are called *Homo habilis*, which means "handy man". *Homo habilis* made rough stone tools from pebbles.

Since the time when *Homo habilis* was alive, a river has cut a deep valley through the land. This valley is called Olduvai Gorge. Fossil remains of both *Homo habilis* and *Australopithecus* have been found at Olduvai.

Stone tool

8 cm long

This is a stone chopper which was made by *Homo habilis*. It is about 1¾ million years old and was found in Olduvai Gorge. *Homo habilis* cut meat with it.

Life at Olduvai

Homo habilis built shelters of branches to protect them from animals and cold winds.

The children probably played and fought as children do today.

The men went hunting and brought their kill back to the camp to share with the others.

1 Going hunting

Homo habilis had a larger brain than *Australopithecus*, and was more intelligent and skilful. They worked together to hunt animals to feed their group.

2

The hunters had no weapons and probably crept up on their prey and then pounced on it. They killed it with stones, or with heavy branches.

3

Stone tools were heavy to carry around, so they were probably made on the spot. The hunters used sharp flakes of stone to cut up the meat to carry it home.

Volcanoes near the lake sometimes erupted and bones were preserved as fossils in the lava.

The women stayed near the camp with the children. They collected eggs, berries and small animals to eat.

Homo habilis was about 1½ m tall

Homo habilis made stone tools by chipping pebbles to give them sharp edges.

If they killed an animal near the camp, the women and children may have run up to share the meat. They ate it raw because they did not know how to make fire.

Palaeontologists have found fossil animal bones which had been cracked open. These show that early people broke open the bones to eat the soft marrow inside.

Make an early man mask

You will need some newspaper, a paper bag, a water-based glue such as wallpaper paste and some wool and paints.

1 BAG STUFFED WITH NEWSPAPER

Mix the glue with water to make a thin paste. Stuff the paper bag with crumpled newspaper and tear the rest of the paper into pieces about the size of your hand.

2 COVER ONE SIDE ONLY

Wet pieces of newspaper in the glue and then paste them flat on to the paper bag. Cover one side of the bag with gluey paper, building it out in the middle.

3 SIDE VIEW

EYE-BROW RIDGE

Mould a nose, lips and eyebrow ridge from lumps of gluey paper. Stick them on to the newspaper on the paper bag and cover with smooth pieces of gluey paper.

4 HOLE FOR STRING

When the newspaper is dry, pull out the paper bag. Then paint the mask and glue on some wool for hair. Pierce two holes for eyes and two holes for the string.

The Fire Makers

Very slowly, as thousands of years went by, the early people evolved and changed. By about a million years ago they were taller and had larger brains than their ancestors.

These people walked upright without stooping and are called *Homo erectus*. They lived between about 1½ million and ¼ million years ago. Fossils of their remains have been found near fire-blackened hearths in caves. These show that by about 300,000 years ago, *Homo erectus* had learned how to make and use fire.

Hunting with fire

Homo erectus frightened animals into an ambush with flaming branches. They caught them with a weapon called a bolas.

The early hominids were terrified by natural fires in the grasslands. The heat, smoke and noise frightened them as it did the other animals.

Gradually the early people learned not to be afraid of fire. They probably took advantage of other animals' fear and caught them as they ran away from the flames.

Homo erectus was about 1½ m tall.

A bolas was made of three round stones wrapped in pieces of skin and tied together with leather thongs. Flung by a hunter, it wrapped round an animal's legs so it fell down.

When they lived

years ago

250,000

1 million — *Homo erectus*

2 million — *Homo habilis*

Australopithecus

The camp fire

Fires helped *Homo erectus* survive in cold weather. His fossil remains have been found in northern China, where the weather was quite cool.

At first *Homo erectus* used fire, but did not know how to make it. They may have taken flaming branches from a forest fire and carried them back to their camp.

With a fire alight in their cave, *Homo erectus* had light and warmth at night. They may have sat around the fire and told hunting stories or made stone tools.

Homo erectus probably noticed that animals which had been burnt in fires were easier to eat than raw meat. So they began to throw meat on the fire to cook it.

Comparing skulls

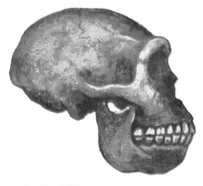

The skull of *Homo erectus* was smaller than that of modern man and like earlier hominids, it had a thick ridge of bone above the eyes and no chin.

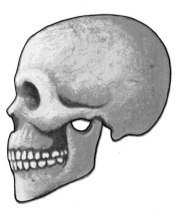

Modern man's skull has a high forehead and pointed chin. The forehead and chin of *Homo erectus* sloped backwards and his brain case was smaller than ours.

Could early people talk?

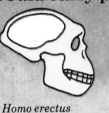

Homo erectus   Modern man

Homo erectus had larger brains than those of earlier hominids, but still not as large as ours. Earlier hominids could not speak, but *Homo erectus* probably grunted sounds and simple words to talk to each other.

A Camp on the Beach

The first *Homo erectus* lived in Africa, but gradually they spread to other parts of the world. A camp site where early people lived over 350,000 years ago has been found in Nice, a town on the south coast of France.

Palaeontologists called this camp site *Terra Amata*, after the street in Nice where it was found. They think a band of *Homo erectus* hunters visited the site every year. They stayed there for only a few days at a time while they hunted animals such as elephants and rhinos.

Wandering hunters

During the year, the band of hunters and their families moved from place to place, following herds of animals. They visited *Terra Amata* in late spring.

Yellow broom flowers in late spring. Palaeontologists found fossil pollen from these flowers in the camp and this shows the time of year when it was built.

Fossil footprint

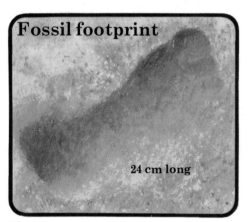

24 cm long

This is the oldest fossil footprint of a human being. A man or woman must have slipped and left a deep heel mark in the mud about 350,000 years ago.

Elephants and rhinos came to drink from the river.

The women probably collected shellfish from the beach and did not go far from the camp.

At *Terra Amata*, palaeontologists found the remains of a wooden hut about nine metres long and five metres wide. They also found stone tools and fossil animal bones.

The early people built the hut from branches with two wooden posts to hold up the roof. There were large rocks beside the hut to protect it from the wind.

Lighting the fire

They probably still did not know how to make fire. They may have carried hot ashes from their old camp fire and used them to light the fire in the new camp.

Near the fire there was a kitchen area where food was prepared and cooked. The people were very untidy and left rubbish and animal bones in the hut.

Prehistoric hearth

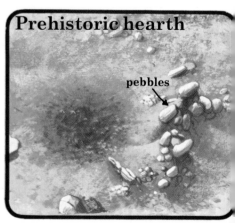

pebbles

This is the hearth where the people lit their fire. They put pebbles round the fire to shield it from the wind and the heat baked and darkened the sand.

Today the sea level is lower and the site of the camp is in the town, not on the beach.

They hunted elephants and rhinos and the deer and fierce wild boars which lived in the forest.

The camp had to be near a fresh water spring because the people had nothing to carry water in.

The people slept on skins near a [fi]re which was kept burning inside [th]e hut. There was also a flat stone [w]here someone sat to make stone [to]ols.

The men went off to hunt animals for the group to eat. They knew that elephants and rhinos came to drink from the river near the camp.

They collected driftwood from the beach to burn on the fire.

Where *Homo erectus* lived

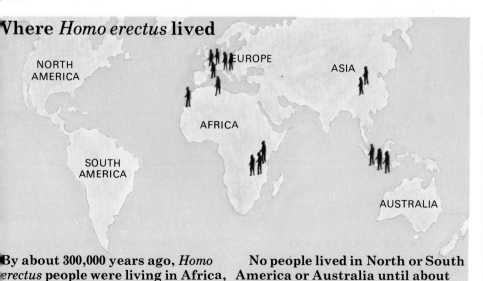

By about 300,000 years ago, *Homo erectus* people were living in Africa, Europe and Asia.

No people lived in North or South America or Australia until about 40,000 years ago.

Was early man hairy?

Man is the only primate who is not very hairy, but scientists do not know when or why people become less hairy.

One result of this is that human mothers have to carry their babies in their arms. Ape babies can cling to their mothers' hair.

An Elephant Hunt

By about half a million years ago, early people had become skilful hunters. Fossils found near a village called Ambrona, in Spain are proof that an elephant hunt took place there about 300,000 years ago.

On this site, palaeontologists found stone tools and the fossil bones of butchered animals. There were also traces of charcoal which showed that fire had been used to frighten the elephants into an ambush. For such a large hunt, several bands of hunters probably joined forces.

The hunters knew that at a certain time every year, a herd of elephants passed through this valley in search of new pastures. So they lay in wait for them.

When they saw the elephants, the men set fire to the grass on the hillsides. The elephants were terrified of the fire and stampeded down the valley.

3 The kill

The more the heavy elephants struggled in the marsh, the deeper they sank in the thick mud. Some of them collapsed, exhausted and the hunters killed them by stabbing them with their pointed wooden spears.

The hunters used tools called hand-axes to cut up the animals. A hand-axe was a stone which was sharpened at one end and held in the palm of the hand.

They probably ate the soft brains and liver of the animal straight away. Then they cut off the rest of the meat and took it back to the camp to cook.

Palaeontologists found an elephant's fossil leg bones and tusk laid in a line. They think the hunters used them as stepping-stones in the wet marsh.

The elephants' escape was blocked by marshy land. With the hunters yelling behind them and fire on either side, the frightened animals rushed into the marsh.

1 Digging up the evidence

Workmen discovered the fossil elephant bones when they were digging a trench. Later palaeontologists visited the site and began to excavate it.

First they used stakes and string to divide the area into squares. Then, very carefully, they removed the earth from each square.

2

They sieved every spadeful of soil to make sure that no evidence was thrown away.

3

Fossil bones and tools were left in place until they had been mapped, numbered and photographed.

4

The fossils were wrapped in plaster to protect them while they were taken to the laboratory.

5

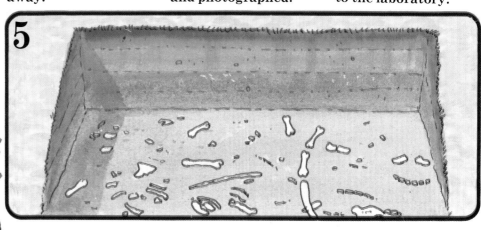

When the diggers had removed all the earth, they found fossil elephant bones, stone hand-axes and charcoal from the fires. There were no human fossils.

The fossil tusk and leg bones which the hunters probably used as a bridge, were in a line across the site. Tests on the soil proved that it had been marshy.

Stone Age Tools

About 2½ million years ago, people first learned how to chip stones to give them sharp cutting edges. These sharpened stones were early man's first tools.

The time when early man lived is called the Palaeolithic Age, which means "Old Stone Age". During this time people made all their tools from stones, bones, wood or antlers. The oldest known tools are called pebble tools. They were very rough but early people gradually became more skilful.

1 Making a tool

First the hunter had to choose a rock. He knew which kinds of rocks made the best tools and sometimes went a long way from the camp looking for good rocks.

2

He used a round pebble as a hammerstone to hit the rock. By carefully aiming his blows he could shape the tool the way he wanted.

Man's special grip

Man can touch his thumb with his middle and index finger. This is called the precision grip. Chimpanzees and other primates can only clench their hands in the power grip.

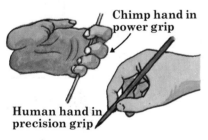

Chimp hand in power grip

Human hand in precision grip

With the precision grip, man can hold things between his fingers. This enables him to make and use fine tools.

Chimps sometimes make and use very simple tools. They pull the leaves off twigs and use them to hook grubs out of termites' nests.

The story of tools

The early hand-axes were used for lots of different jobs. Later people made different tools for special purposes and stopped making hand-axes.

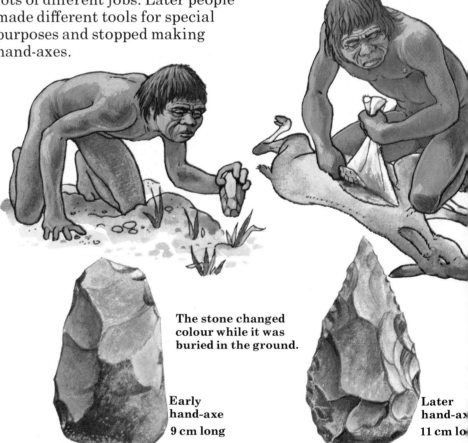

The stone changed colour while it was buried in the ground.

Early hand-axe 9 cm long

Later hand-axe 11 cm long

About a million years ago, people made large hand-axes with blunt ends. The edges were not very finely flaked and these tools were used for digging and for cutting up animals.

This sharp-edged hand-axe was made about 300,000 years ago. Its edges were very finely flaked. It was used for stripping the skins off animals and for cutting and scraping meat from bones.

3

he tool maker knocked several rge chips off the rock to make the ough shape of the tool. If the rock roke in the wrong place he had to tart again.

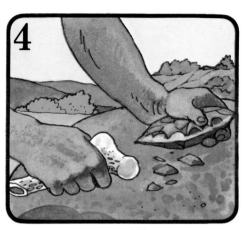

4

Next he used an animal's bone as a hammer to chip small flakes from the edge of the rock. This gave the tool a very thin, sharp edge. The flakes were used to cut meat.

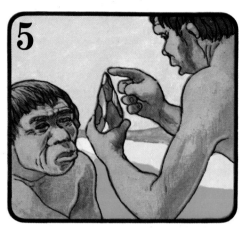

5

The finished tool is called a hand-axe. It had a pointed end, a thin cutting edge and a rounded base which was held in the palm of the hand.

Scraper
5 cm long

radually, early people learned ow to shape flakes of rock into ifferent kinds of tools. This is a ool called a hollow scraper which as used to sharpen sticks to ake spears.

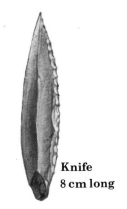

Knife
8 cm long

About 40,000 years ago, people made sharp, knife-like blades from flakes of rock. They also made chisel-like tools called burins for shaping needles or spearheads from antler.

Tool time chart

This chart shows when some of the different kinds of Stone Age tools were made.

years ago

10,000

Blades

50,000

Later hand-axes

200,000

Early hand-axes

1 million

Choppers

Pebble tools

2½ million

The Palaeolithic, or Old Stone Age, lasted from 2½ million years ago until 10,000 years ago. About 40,000 years ago, people stopped making hand-axes and made all their tools from flakes of rock.

Neanderthal Man

By about 250,000 years ago, *Homo erectus* had evolved and changed and become a new kind of people. These new people are included in the same group as modern man and are called *Homo sapiens*.

In the past there were several different kinds of *Homo sapiens*, but today there is only one. One of the early kinds of *Homo sapiens* is called Neanderthal man. Neanderthal people lived during the ice age, about 50,000 years ago, when large parts of the world were covered with ice.

Hunting in the ice age

Neanderthal people were short and stocky with large muscles. They were very strong and were the first people to adapt to living in in very cold places.

The people hunted animals such as woolly mammoths with wooden spears. They ate its meat and used its skin and thick shaggy hair to keep them warm.

Neanderthal skull

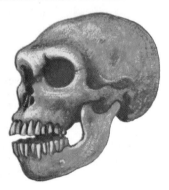

The skulls of Neanderthal people had thick brow ridges and large teeth. The backs were pointed but the brains were the same size as modern man's brain.

Tools

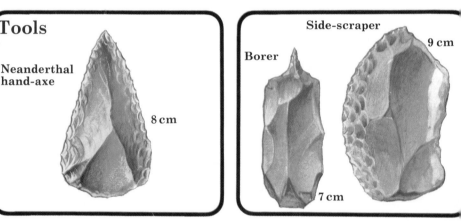

Neanderthal hand-axe

8 cm

Side-scraper

Borer

9 cm

7 cm

Neanderthal people were skilful at making tools. Their hand-axes were smaller and easier to manage than those of earlier people such as *Homo erectus*.

They made stone scrapers for cleaning the fat from animal skins and borers for making holes. The scraper had a round edge for scraping and a straight edge to hol

Cooking

Neanderthal people may have cooked meat on flat stones. First they lit a fire on the stones to heat them.

When the stones were hot the fire was swept away and the meat was thrown onto the hot stones.

The heat from the stones slowly roasted the meat. This made it tender and easier to chew.

1 Model cave

You will need a paper bag, som newspaper, water-based glue, such as wallpaper paste, and plasticine and paints.

DIP PAPER IN GLUE

Stuff the paper bag with newspape and cover one side of it with pieces of newspaper soaked in glue, as described on page 73. Leave it to d for several hours.

A Neanderthal home

Neanderthal people lived in caves or built huts from branches covered with animal skins. Sometimes they built huts inside the damp, cold caves or in the shelter of an overhanging rock.

To make clothes from animal skins they first had to remove the fat from the inside of the skin. They pegged the skin taut on the ground and cleaned it with a stone scraper.

They may have dried the skins in smoke from the fire to keep them soft and leathery. Then they pierced holes in the edge of the skin with a pointed stone borer.

They probably wrapped themselves in the skins and threaded leather thongs through the holes to join the edges. They may have bound their feet in skins too.

2

TRIM WITH SCISSORS TO MAKE A STRAIGHT EDGE

When the newspaper is quite dry, pull out the paper bag to leave the hollow cave. You can paint the cave and put a cave painting inside like those on page 88.

3

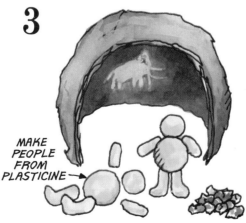

MAKE PEOPLE FROM PLASTICINE →

To make plasticine cave people, shape the body, legs, arms and head from plasticine and press them together. Stick bits of gravel in their hands as tools.

4

STICKY TAPE

GRAVEL

You could make a model fire from twigs and red paper and sprinkle earth on the cave floor. To make trees, tape some leafy twigs to the outside of the cave.

83

Cave Bear Magic

1

Neanderthal people hunted fierce cave bears. They believed that the bears' skulls and bones could make magic and probably thought this magic would keep them safe.

2

To catch the bear they followed its footprints back to the cave where it lived. It was a dangerous hunt because the bears were over $3\frac{1}{2}$ m long and very fierce.

3

They probably threw burning branches into the cave to smoke out the bear. The hunters waited outside with their wooden spears tipped with stone.

4

The angry bear came rushing out of the smoky cave and the hunters leapt at it with their spears. Others probably threw heavy rocks at the animal. Some of the men may have been killed in the fight.

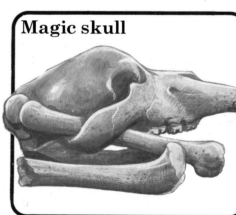

5

When the bear was dead, they cut off its head and carried it back to their cave. They put the head in a pit with the skulls of bears killed in other hunts.

Magic skull

This skull of a cave bear was found in a cave where Neanderthal people lived. They had put the leg bone of a young bear into the skull of an older bear to make magic.

Burying the Dead

The first people spent most of their time hunting and collecting food. They probably never wondered how life began, or what happened to them when they died.

Neanderthal people seem to have been the first to bury their dead. Palaeontologists have found skeletons buried in graves in the earthy floors of caves where Neanderthal people lived. The bodies were sometimes buried with tools which perhaps they believed they would need in their next lives.

This is the entrance to a large cave in the mountains of Iraq. Inside, palaeontologists found the grave of a 40-year-old man who died about 60,000 years ago.

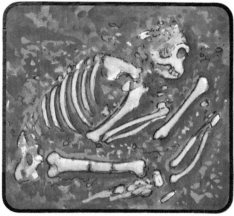

The man's bones were preserved as fossils by the weight of the earth on top of them. He had been laid curled-up in the grave with his knees under his chin.

It must have taken a long time to dig a hole in the earthy floor of the cave. The Neanderthal people had only pointed stone tools and sticks to dig with.

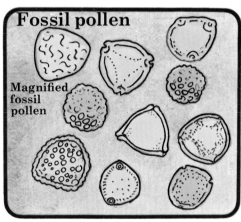

Fossil pollen

Magnified fossil pollen

Scientists found fossil pollen in the grave which showed that the man had been buried with flowers. This is what pollen looks like under a microscope.

Flowers for the grave

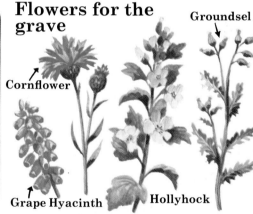

Groundsel

Cornflower

Grape Hyacinth

Hollyhock

These are the kinds of wild flowers which were in the man's grave. They still grow in parts of Europe, so you may be able to find them.

The burial

The Neanderthal people laid the dead man on some pine branches and scattered wild flowers from the hills over his body.

The First Modern People

Neanderthal people died out about 40,000 years ago and a new kind of *Homo sapiens* evolved. These new people were the first to have the same shaped skulls and bodies as modern man. They are called the Cro-Magnon people and were our direct ancestors.

Cro-Magnon people lived in caves or huts towards the end of the last ice age. The weather was cold and snowy and only short grass and shrubs could grow. The people hunted reindeer and woolly mammoths.

1 Hunting and fishing

Cro-Magnon people made many new kinds of tools and weapons. They tied antler points, with barbs pointing backwards, on their spears to wound animals.

They used spear throwers to help them throw spears further. The spear throwers were carved from antler and some were decorated with carved patterns.

Sewing

Needles made from antler were found with the remains of Cro-Magnon people. This shows that they sewed skins.

Cro-Magnon people used a chisel-shaped stone tool called a burin to cut the antler. They were probably the first people to make needles and sew.

They bored a hole in the tip of the needle to make an eye. Then they smoothed the sides and point by rubbing the needle on a piece of stone.

They probably used a stone borer to make holes in the leather so they could push the needle through. They sewed with thin strips of leather or gut.

Cro-Magnon people often stitched little beads of coloured rock to their clothes to decorate them. Sometimes they used shells with holes in them too.

Ancient burial

Many graves of Cro-Magnon people have been found in the floors of huts and caves. This skeleton was covered with beads and shells from the clothes which had rotted away.

Cro-Magnon skull

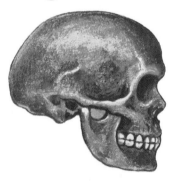

This is the skull of a Cro-Magnon woman. It is the same shape as skulls of modern people and has a large, rounded brain-case, a pointed chin and upright forehead

They caught fish with harpoons which were carved from antlers and had backward-pointing barbs. They tied the harpoons on to spears and stabbed the fish with them.

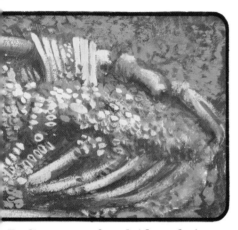

Bodies were often laid on their sides in the graves, with their knees pulled up to their chins. Sometimes there were tools and weapons in the graves too.

When they lived

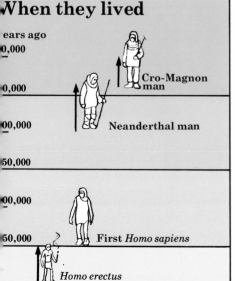

years ago

0,000	Cro-Magnon man
00,000	Neanderthal man
50,000	
00,000	First *Homo sapiens*
50,000	
	Homo erectus

Mammoth bone huts

Some Cro-Magnon people lived on the cold, flat steppe lands of eastern Europe. There were no caves to live in and few trees for wood to build huts. They hunted woolly mammoths which provided nearly everything they needed.

They built huts from mammoths' long leg bones and tusks, covered with skins. They stood the bones in skulls, because they could not push them into the frozen ground.

These Cro-Magnon people wore trousers and jackets made from mammoth skins. They ate mammoth meat and stored it in pits dug in the cold ground.

Make cave man's necklaces

Cro-Magnon people made necklaces from little stones and shells, fishbones or bits of eggshell. They probably threaded seeds and fruit pips too, but these have rotted away.

PAINT THE PIPS AND SHELLS

Sea-shells and stones often have little holes in them. If you visit the seaside you could collect them and thread them on thin string for a necklace.

You can also pierce little bits of fresh eggshell with a needle. Thread them on cotton to make a necklace with apple and orange pips.

Cave Painting

In the depths of their caves, Cro-Magnon people painted pictures of the animals they hunted. They were probably the first people to discover how to paint and use colour, though Neanderthal people may have decorated their bodies with a powdered red rock called ochre.

Cro-Magnon people may have painted the pictures to make magic. Perhaps they believed that the pictures would keep them safe and help them catch the animals they hunted for food.

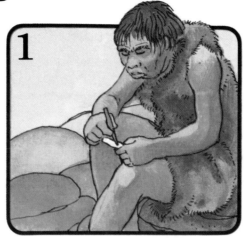

No remains have been found of pictures painted by earlier people. They probably painted and scratched patterns on bits of wood which have rotted away.

Cro-Magnon people painted pictures of horses, bison and reindeer. Often they put spears in the paintings as magic to make their own spears kill the real animals.

Magic carvings

Cro-Magnon people carved figures in stone of very fat or pregnant women. They also modelled statues in clay and dried them in the fire.

The people may have believed that carvings like this would bring them good fortune.

Painting the caves

Cave paintings by Cro-Magnon people have been found in France and Spain. The colours are still very bright, although they were painted over 30,000 years ago.

The early cave paintings were always of animals and hunting scenes, so it was probably the men who painted them.

They lit the cave with lamps made by burning fur or moss soaked in animal fat.

The paints were made from coloured soft rocks. They ground the rocks to a powder between a bone and a stone and mixed the powder with animal fat.

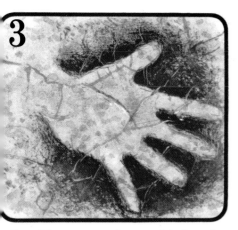

3

A Cro-Magnon artist put his hand on the rock and then blew paint round it through a reed. There are few pictures of people or plants in the early paintings.

4

This engraving on a rock wall shows a woolly mammoth with its long, shaggy hair. Cave art often shows us what the prehistoric animals looked like.

Make a cave painting

You will need some plaster of Paris, a box such as a large size matchbox, a piece of string, sticky tape and paints.

1

MAKE ENDS OF STRING STICK UP

STICKY TAPE

Take a bit of string about 6 cm long and fold it in half to make a loop. Tape the loop end of the string on to the bottom of the box on the inside.

2

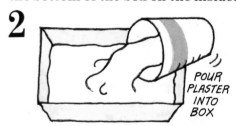

POUR PLASTER INTO BOX

Mix the plaster of Paris with water to make a thin paste and pour it into the box to make a layer about about 3 cm deep. Leave it to dry and then tear the box off the plaster.

3

Copy or trace one of the cave paintings on this page on to the slab of plaster. Then paint it, using the same colours as the cave men: red, yellow, brown and black.

4

CARVED LINES

You could also make a cave man's engraving. Copy the shape of the woolly mammoth in box three on to a plaster slab. Then carve the lines with an old fork.

Sometimes they painted the outline of the animal first and then filled it in with moss or fur pads soaked in paint.

They stored the paint in hollow bones with lumps of fat in the ends. There was no green or blue paint as these colours were not found in the rocks.

The artists made brushes from animal hair tied to small bones. Sometimes they put the paint on with their fingers, or used little pads of fur or moss.

Hunters in the Forest

The ice age ended about 10,000 years ago and the weather became warmer. In northern Europe trees and forests grew again. The animals, such as mammoths and woolly rhinos which had lived during the ice age, died out. The people living then looked very like modern people.

At about this time, people in the Middle East learned how to plant seeds and to farm. In Europe they still hunted for their food and used bows and arrows for the first time.

Lakeside village

The remains of camps where hunters lived about 10,000 years ago have been found in Denmark and England.

Piles of broken tools, animal bones, fish bones and shells were found near the camp. These rubbish heaps are called middens.

The people hollowed out tree trunks with their axes to make boats. The remains of several boats have been found.

They shot ducks and other birds with arrows. They ate the meat and used the feathers on their arrows.

Arrows and axes

flint
Arrow head
resin
antler
Axe head 8 cm long
8 cm long
Fish hooks

The hunters made axes by fixing sharp, chipped stones into hollow antlers. These were joined to wooden handles. They chopped down trees with these axes.

People often camped near lakes in clearings in the forest. Where the ground was wet and muddy, they built their houses on platforms of tree trunks.

They cut down trees to build their houses and covered the branches with skins to keep out the rain. The ground was damp so they covered it with bark.

1 Going fishing

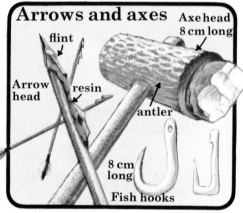

Remains of a fish trap about 1 m long

This is the remains of a fish trap which was found in a marsh in Denmark. The people ate lots of fish which they caught in traps, or with harpoons or hooks.

2

They made the fish trap from the long, thin branches of willow trees. They peeled the bark off the branches and wove them together in the shape of baskets.

3

They cut down trees to build their houses and covered the branches with skins to keep out the rain. The ground was damp so they covered it with bark.

To catch the fish the hunters built a dam across a stream. They put the trap in an opening in the dam. When the fish swam through they were caught in the trap.

The women collected fruits and berries from the forest.

The hunters had tame dogs to help them chase and kill wild animals.

Hunting in the forest was always difficult and dangerous. The men hunted red deer, roe deer and wild pigs. Bows and arrows were the best weapons to use in the forest.

The tips and barbs of arrows were tiny flakes of stone, glued on with resin. This is the sap from birch trees. Feathers balanced the arrows in flight.

Rock paintings

These paintings were done about 10,000 years ago in Spain. Unlike earlier paintings they show human figures. The man is shooting deer with a bow and arrow.

This is a rock painting of a woman collecting honey from a bees' nest in a tree. The bees are shown swarming angrily round their nest.

The first dogs

Dogs are descended from wolves. They probably first became tame when wolf cubs were caught by hunters and taken back to their camps. Wolves live in packs and the strongest wolf is its leader. If a wolf grows up amongst people it is obedient to its human master.

The First Farmers

In the Middle East, about 11,000 years ago, people discovered that they could sow the seeds of wild plants and grow the crops they needed.

These people were the first farmers. They planted wheat and looked after sheep and goats which had become tame. They had a constant supply of food and no longer had to move around the countryside, hunting animals and collecting plants to eat. They built villages near their land and settled down to farm it.

In the warm, dry lands of the Middle East, wheat grew wild on the hills. People collected the grain of the wheat as well as fruit and nuts to eat.

They carried the wheat back to their camp and ground it between two stones to make flour. Some of the wheat probably fell on the ground and grew near their huts.

The first farm animals

The wild ancestors of sheep, goats, pigs and cattle lived in the Middle East. They became the first farm animals.

The people hunted these animals and sometimes carried young lambs or goat kids back to the village.

The young animals became tame. Their babies were tame too and soon the village had a herd of animals.

The farmers looked after their herds and protected them from wild animals. They drank the milk from the animals and killed them when they wanted meat or skins. They no longer needed to hunt wild animals.

Farming village

The walls of the houses were made from a mixture of mud and straw which had dried and hardened in the sun. Rain damaged the walls and they had to be repaired after the winter. The roofs were thatched with straw covered with mud.

3

4

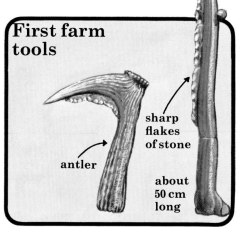

sharp
flakes
of stone

antler

about
50 cm
long

The people noticed that wheat plants grew from fallen seeds. They tried scattering seeds on land which they cleared near their camp and waited for plants to grow.

They collected the ripened wheat and had enough grain to last them for several months. They made tools, called sickles, for cutting the stalks of the wheat.

The farmers' sickles were made from flakes of flint fixed in handles. The handles were made of wood or from the jaw bone or antler of an animal.

Some of the houses had several rooms and the floors were covered with mats woven from rushes. One of the buildings was a store house, or granary, for the wheat. In the courtyard of the houses there was a large oven which was built of dried mud.

Baking bread

In the yard outside the houses there was a large oven where the women baked bread. The oven was made of dried mud and a fire was lit inside.

The women ground the wheat to make coarse brown flour. They mixed the flour with water and shaped the dough into flat, round loaves. The loaves were baked on stones heated in the oven and the bread was thin and hard.

Time Chart:
The Stone Age

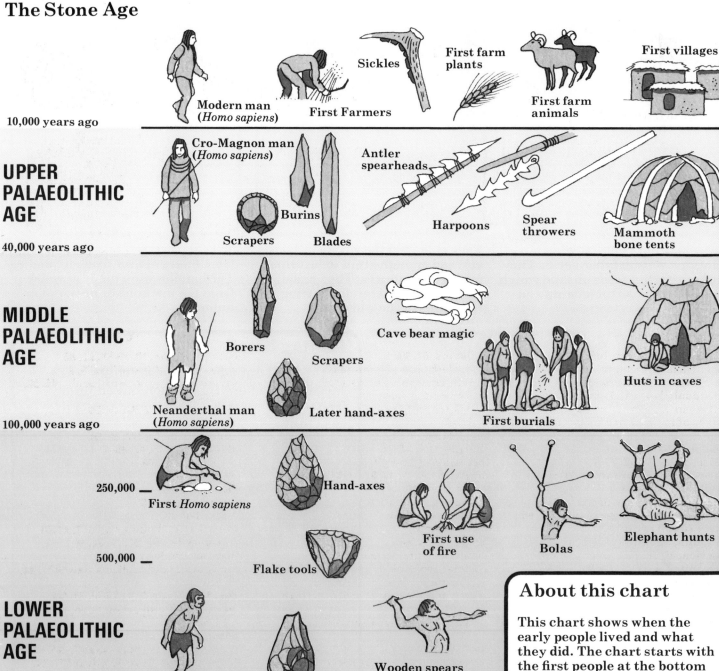

10,000 years ago

Modern man (*Homo sapiens*)
First Farmers
Sickles
First farm plants
First farm animals
First villages

UPPER PALAEOLITHIC AGE

40,000 years ago

Cro-Magnon man (*Homo sapiens*)
Scrapers
Burins
Blades
Antler spearheads
Harpoons
Spear throwers
Mammoth bone tents

MIDDLE PALAEOLITHIC AGE

100,000 years ago

Neanderthal man (*Homo sapiens*)
Borers
Scrapers
Later hand-axes
Cave bear magic
First burials
Huts in caves

250,000 —

First *Homo sapiens*
Hand-axes
First use of fire
Bolas
Elephant hunts

500,000 —

Flake tools

LOWER PALAEOLITHIC AGE

Homo erectus
Early hand-axes
Wooden spears

1 million —

Homo habilis
Pebble tools
Shelters of branches

First *Homo*
Australopithecus
Oldest tools

2½ million years ago

About this chart

This chart shows when the early people lived and what they did. The chart starts with the first people at the bottom and works upwards to the more recent people. Palaeontologists' time charts are like this because this is how they find the fossils. The oldest fossils are in the deepest layers of rock with the newer fossils above.

The Palaeolithic or Old Stone Age, is divided into three parts: the lower, middle and upper. On this chart the sizes of the different parts are not to scale. The names and dates of the different ages of early man are at the side.

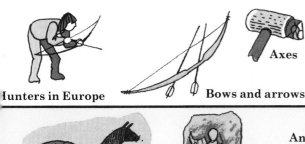
Hunters in Europe

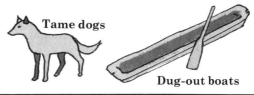
Bows and arrows
Axes
Tame dogs

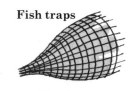
Dug-out boats
Fish traps

Cave paintings

Carved figures

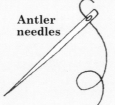
Antler needles

Jewellery

Sewn clothes

ndex

In this index, the English meanings of the Latin and Greek scientific names are in brackets. The names of individual plants and animals are written in *italics* and the names of groups of animals are in ordinary type.